Diary of an Affair

ALSO BY JEANNIE SAKOL

Fiction:

FLORA SWEET

MOTHERS & LOVERS

MAIDEN VOYAGE

NEW YEAR'S EVE

I WAS NEVER THE PRINCESS

GUMDROP, GUMDROP LET DOWN YOUR HAIR

Non-Fiction:

KENNEDY: THE NEW GENERATION (TEXT)

THE WONDERFUL WORLD OF COUNTRY MUSIC

THE INEPT SEDUCER

(with co-author Caroline Latham)

THE ROYALS A-TO-Z

THE KENNEDY FAMILY

E FOR ELVIS

Diary of an Affair

by

JEANNIE SAKOL

DONALD I. FINE, INC.
New York

 Published in the United States of America by Donald I. Fine, Inc. and in Canada by General Publishing Company Limited.

Library of Congress Cataloging-in-Publication Data

Sakol, Jeannie.
Diary of an affair.

I. Title.
PS3569.A455D53 1989 813'.54 88-45875
ISBN 1-55611-136-3
Manufactured in the United States of America
10 9 8 7 6 5 4 3 2 1

Designed by Irving Perkins Associates

For Pat Miller, especially.
And for Donna Jackson, Rosemarie Lennon, Meg Siesfeld,
David English, Robert Smith, Ruth and Paul Nathan,
Don Fine and Susan Schwartz.
They all know why.
And for the man in the purple sweats I met early one
summer morning at the Central Park reservoir, who doesn't.

March, 1989

Diary of an Affair

Liza

Here I go again. I'm at my desk, gorging a cheese Danish and hot chocolate instead of my usual rice cake and decaf, wondering why I'm doing this to myself. But it isn't the calories I'm thinking about. It's the guy in the purple sweat suit I ran into earlier this morning in Central Park—literally ran into, that is, on the jogging track at the reservoir.

It was my fault. I slipped on some wet leaves. Yet he was the one who apologized: "Sorry. You okay?" He didn't wait for an answer. No move to pick me up or start a conversation. His eyes met mine for a split second, nervously, like I was going to punch him out. His face was damp and flushed with exertion. Men look better than women do when they sweat. Not fair, but what is? As he turned away, I noticed the backs of his ears turn red. Maybe he found me as attractive as I found him.

Suddenly, I was incredibly turned on, a Mount St. Helens volcano ready to blow. Suddenly, I wanted to run after him and take him by surprise; throw him a glance over my shoulder and entice him to a lover's cave in the underbrush . . . and there on a mound of velvet moss kiss him all over and tease him till he begged for mercy, and then take him on a roller coaster ride to the center of my universe. And watch his face when he exploded.

Suddenly, I was feeling something besides numb from the neck down. In the year since the divorce, nature's novocaine has deadened the pain while my wounds healed. Maybe the bad time is finally over. Maybe there is someone new on the horizon, the mythic stranger appearing from out of the blue.

You never know when or where or how you're going to meet the next significant someone in your life; it could happen at the airport, the health club, or the popcorn line at the movies.

I met Mark at Bloomingdale's. The way he told it later he picked me up. Of course it was the other way around. It all happened four years ago, just after I left Eileen Ford to start my own talent agency. I was early for my appointment with the special events director and cruising the men's department on the main floor when I spotted this man with thick hair and football shoulders trying on jackets. Clearly, I thought, this man should not be permitted to shop by himself.

He had on a racetrack check that looked like he sold dirty pictures for a living, and he was actually considering it when I caught his eye in the mirror and shook my head negative. The next one was a mustard tweed, Prince Charles on the moors. Better? I bit my lip in exaggerated concentration and then did a slow Gallic shrug. Better, but not quite there. Third time up was a hit. Gray is gray, but this particular gray was like a photographer's filter. It brought the planes of his face into sharp focus—the high cheekbones, prominent nose, and truly dangerous mouth. His pale blue polyester eyes turned vivid cobalt and piercing.

I sighed theatrically, hand clutched to heaving breast, and nodded my approval. The result excited him. "Don't quit on me now. I need some slacks, too. Can I possibly induce you to come with me while I take off my pants?"

Cute? I could be cute, too.

"Not on the first date."

And so we were married. For two years of fast-lane bliss, we became that bright, successful young New York couple that's celebrated in magazines and TV commercials—until the night I got back early from a location shoot and found him in our bed with Tiffany Thomas.

My friends said I was better off without him, but I shouldn't rush into a divorce because a good man was hard to find. My mother said thank God we had no children, but maybe it was my fault, men were men, they had *needs,* and maybe I should give him another chance because a good man was hard to find.

I said forget it. My career was now the most important thing in my life—money, power, independence—and no man was ever going to get to me again. I would live alone, give dinner parties, help worthy causes, and go to museums. Henceforth, a man would be used for decorative purposes only or as a recreational vehicle on weekends. I was sadly convinced that a good, loving, honest, and mutually supportive relationship was impossible.

Until this morning in Central Park. This stranger pushed my ON button. I could feel a high-voltage rush of energy as I raced home to shower and change—scattering pigeons, frightening squirrels, tap dancing on benches, vaulting fences.

Today, I could rule the world and make it a better place for everyone. I wanted everyone to be happy and excited. Everyone. My street radar, on the blink since the divorce, was sending out signals again. I was back on screen. A cabdriver whistled. A dog-walker blew me kisses. A black dude in spandex and shades crooned the ultimate accolade: "Foxy!"

I was so juiced, I couldn't wait for the elevator. I thundered up ten flights of stairs like a mountain goat in heat. The ice-cold shower reminded me of the waterfall Mark and I found in New England. With the water sluicing through my hair and down my breasts, I threw back my head and howled, *"Go fuck yourself, Mark. Today's my day!"*

Today's my day. Heading down Park Avenue to my office, the city was still morning fresh and fragrant. New York had never looked so beautiful and rich with possibility. I'm on a roll, I thought, the force is with me.

Today I will finalize the Revlon deal for Athena. She's my first discovery. I've been coaching her and training her and now she's ready for the big time. I found her two years ago at a Greek street fair in Brooklyn. She was eating souvlaki. Her hair was hanging down her back below her waist. Her face was a Greek coin, her nose descending straight down from her forehead with no bridge. She had no figure to speak of, no curves; just long, lean lines, long legs, long arms, a long neck like a swan's. Three men watched her lick her lips of *tahini* and onions. No question about it. She had The Look.

She was my first discovery after leaving Eileen Ford to set up on my own. Eileen taught me everything I know. She could afford to go scouting for talent in Scandinavia and the Orient. I could afford only Brooklyn; and as it has turned out, Brooklyn is all I've needed.

Athena's mother, Irini, thought I was a madam on a recruitment drive until I explained about my agency, about how much Brooke Shields and Paulina Porizkova earn, and invited them both to my office. Irini is a vacuum cleaner. She appropriated all the pens from my desk, asked me if she could call her sister in Athens to discuss the matter—my phone, my expense—and suggested a limo to take them back to Brooklyn, since it was a rush hour and the subway was crowded.

She supports my conviction that all models should be orphans, bred on Model Farms. Some girls look that way, unreal, no pores, as though if you unzipped their chests you'd find foam rubber stuffing.

The girl's full name was Alexandra Maria Athena Georgopoulos. I like the impact of a single name: Wilhelmina. Iman. Twiggy. Veruschka. Cher. Henceforth and forthwith, she would be Athena, a goddess of style if not wisdom.

I was lucky to find her that day. Then it was up to me to turn the possibility into a reality. Life is a merry-go-round, Athena my first gold ring. I have a good, long reach. Nobody's going to give it to you; you have to stretch out and grab it yourself.

The same thing applies to the man in the park. Something definitely happened to me this morning. A stranger touched my arm. I think something happened to him, too. His ears turned red. Am I crazy or something? Too much oxygen to the brain? I'll know better tomorrow if he shows up at the reservoir looking for me.

Daniel

I felt light-headed all the way home from the park. It wasn't the jogging—although I'm still getting used to this new exercise regimen—it was that girl in yellow! She literally knocked me over. Well, almost. I was just plugging along, thinking what lousy shape I'm in, and suddenly she fell against me like a ton of bricks. We both lost our balance, but I managed to keep us on our feet. It was funny how we both laughed and apologized.

"My fault."

"No, my fault."

"No, my fault."

"I insist, my fault."

She looked so adorable, so fresh and young and adorable, that I had this crazy urge to scoop her up in my arms and give her a big wet kiss.

Maybe it's mid-life crisis like Maggie says. I'll be forty-five next month, but I can still feel the teenage thrill of it all. Her hair was wild and loose, she smelled so good, like cinnamon or flowers, and her skin—no makeup, just this shiny glow. She reminded me of the girls at my first college mixer. I wanted to be Mr. Suave and introduce myself, but I got all tongue-tied—what Jennifer and her girlfriends call a nerd. Daddy was a nerd, Jennifer, he couldn't talk to the pretty lady. What an idiot.

I could feel my ears burning like they always do when I'm under stress. Maybe it's my imagination, but when I continued jogging I could feel her eyes on me. I was a kid again on the campus track, showing off for the girls. I could feel myself straighten up and try to look taller. And younger. What a nerd.

Maggie had breakfast waiting for me.

"You okay?" She thinks jogging is dangerous for a "man of my age."

"I'm starved."

I realized she was waiting for me to peck her on the cheek as I always do on arrival home. Was I that rattled by a chance encounter in the park? Maggie looked composed and well-scrubbed as usual, her hair scraped back tight in the tortoise-shell barrette, wearing the crisp checked shirt and khaki jeans from L. L. Bean. Always the same. I don't think I've ever seen her disheveled. She was a model when I met her, and she looks exactly the same. Metabolism, she says. She can knock back a quart of chocolate chip ice cream and never gain an ounce. A genuine cause for divorce, I once said as a joke. She looked so frightened that I realized it was a bad joke.

Sometimes I wonder if she's ever regretted giving up her career, even though she insists it was just showroom stuff, not big time like magazines and TV. Sometimes when I see her and

Jennifer on their bicycles it's hard to tell mother from daughter. She's still beautiful after all these years of marriage and two children, and I still love her as much as I did the day we got married. So why was I feeling so guilty, and why was I so nervous when she asked a perfectly ordinary question about how things went in the park?

"Fine."

"Just fine?"

I couldn't think of anything to add. I changed the subject. "The kids leave for school?"

We both knew they had.

She looked at me quizzically and then smiled. "Eat your oatmeal, silly."

My uneasiness must have showed. She reached out and touched my face with uncharacteristic tenderness. We love each other, but we are not overly demonstrative. "Maybe jogging is a good idea, after all," she said. "You look very young, almost boyish. And very handsome, darling."

While I dressed for work, she filled me in about Jennifer's flute lessons and Sandi's part in the school play and her own ceramics class and the committee to plant new trees. I filled her in about the forthcoming seminar for New York travel agents and how my speech was going to call for more industry cooperation and less cutthroat competition so we could all survive and prosper.

"What does Sonia say about that?"

Maggie's got a bee in her bonnet about Sonia. She wants me to dissolve the partnership and go out on my own.

"About what?"

"About less cutthroat competition."

When I first started out in the travel business, I was working for Sonia, one of the tough old-timers. She knows every trick in the book and some that have never been tried. Even before computers, she had a photographic mind. She could recite every flight schedule of every carrier from here to Melbourne, and every discount, off-season, or group booking permutation you could name. When I became a partner, the idea was she would retire and retain a percentage. That was fifteen years ago, and she's still in the office before anyone else and still there at night when the staff leaves after what she calls "a half day."

Her husband died young, leaving her the business. There was never any question of a romance between us; she treats me more like a son. I have to admit Sonia can be a card-carrying bitch. Half the time she treats Maggie as if she's invisible. Then she tries to make up for it by buying her expensive gifts that are totally wrong for her, like a maribou housecoat from Bendel's with the five-hundred-dollar price tag still attached and marked Not Returnable.

"Why shouldn't I talk about cutthroat competition?"

"Because Sonia invented cutthroat competition. You yourself said she's cut more throats than Jack the Ripper."

I had to laugh. She was right, Sonia was known throughout the industry for drawing blood. Good old reliable Maggie. I would have looked like a horse's ass. I would stick to industry cooperation and let it go at that.

The office was chaos as usual when I got there, all the computer terminals on overload, phones ringing off the hook, Sonia bellowing threats and endearments, messengers lined up to rush airline tickets and vouchers to waiting clients. I love the travel business. It's fast and furious. Profits depend on split-second decisions on special rates, off-season discounts, currency fluctuations, and bulk bookings. It demands total concentration and the ability to digest and evaluate constantly changing data. Yet throughout the day, my thoughts kept drifting to Central Park and the girl in yellow.

I was filled with a yearning for something I could not define. I felt deprived of a joy I have never known. I could not stop wondering who she was and whether she would be at the reservoir tomorrow morning and what I would say when I saw her again and what she would say to me, assuming she even remembered me. Of course she would remember me, at least I think she would remember meeting me this morning, wouldn't she?

Who am I kidding? This whole thing is ridiculous. I'm a happily married man. I love my wife and children. I don't play around. I like my life just the way it is—or was, until this morning. Frankly, I'm scared to death for what I've been thinking all day—crazy thoughts, thoughts that could destroy a marriage and wreck your life.

Maggie and I have built a strong marriage on a strong foundation. In just one day, it feels like a house of cards swaying in the wind of change. The best thing I can do is regard this morning as a passing aberration and erase it from my mind. Nothing happened and it's up to me to see that nothing does.

Central Park is not the only place to run. Tomorrow, I'll go to Riverside Drive instead. I feel better knowing I've made the right decision. Why look for trouble? You can't have everything; and yet, and yet . . . I can't remember feeling so young and alive with desire.

On the way home for dinner, I bought Maggie a bouquet of flowers.

"What's the occasion?" she protested, though it was clear that she was pleased.

"Watch it, Mom!" Jennifer was scrutinizing us with adolescent know-it-all insinuation. "When husbands bring home flowers, they've got a guilty conscience!"

"Jennifer!" I exploded, certain my guilt was written all over me.

Maggie merely laughed. "She watches too many soap operas. Jennifer, apologize to your father. That was an unkind and silly thing to say."

Liza

I must be out of my mind. I got to the park early. I don't usually wear mascara to jog, but this morning I did. I kept thinking, Where is he? Any second now, I'll see him. Any second he'll be here. I ran around the reservoir twice, once in each direction, so there was no way of missing him. I hung around until after nine o'clock, figuring any minute I would see him, any minute he'd show up.

Maybe he's sick. Maybe he got hit by a truck. Maybe I made the whole thing up. I couldn't have made the whole thing up. Something definitely happened. Maybe he's shy, a brilliant mathematician but lacking social skills. Maybe I should have said, "Let's lunch," and given him my card. I don't carry cards to the park. From now on, maybe I should. Why am I putting myself through this shit? I can just see myself hitting on guys in the park with my business card.

What I should really do is have my head examined. He probably has an IQ of ten and wears white socks with clocks and a pencil case clipped to his shirt pocket and is married with six kids and just got laid off in a corporate takeover.

Ah well, it was swell while it lasted; sing no sad songs for me. At least he jolted me out of the blahs. Yesterday I sashayed into the Revlon conference room with fire in my belly and my butter-melt smile. These are tough cookies. I keep a pair of spike-heel shoes to wear for just such negotiations. They make me feel incredibly belligerent when I'm scared to death, and they intimidate men. Once I've made my entrance, sat down on a straight-back chair—soft sofas swallow you alive—and crossed my legs, I speak very softly. I've learned that then the enemy has to lean forward in order to hear me. That knocks them off balance and that's when I get what I want. Or at least, that's my theory—sometimes it works.

What Revlon wanted was Athena to launch their new Classique Beauty line—"ageless beauty for women of every age." On their terms.

What I wanted was my terms, including escalators into the twenty-first century.

Things had reached an impasse, at which point I thought it prudent to mention a certain Japanese consortium's plan to launch a competitive fragrance and cosmetics line in the United States. "They want Athena, too—exclusively."

This information made them cranky as hell, but a little while later I emerged a star. I had made a quantum leap into the big time. I had been lucky enough to find Athena when she was fourteen and smart enough to sign her to an exclusive management contract. Soon she would be as familiar as Isabella Rossellini and Brooke Shields, with movies and endorsements to come. Eat your heart out, Eileen Ford. Watch my speed, Johnny Casablancas. I'm carving out my piece of the pie.

As usual when I've finished a rough negotiation, I suffer a severe energy dip. The adrenalin has run out. I need sweets. Today, back at Liza Central, I kick off the high heels and ask

Myrna, my new secretary, to get me The Regular, a cheese Danish and a hot chocolate, my favorite fix. Myrna regards me with schoolgirl awe, which is intensely annoying, since she's twenty-six and I'm only five years older.

I should be on top of the world. I *am* on top of the world. The way things are going, next year I can open the West Coast branch and make that reciprocal deal with London.

So why do I feel so deflated, like someone jabbed a pin in my party balloon? The question is rhetorical. I know what's got me close to tears. It's seven o'clock and I'm on my way home to change into something high-power sleek for tonight's AIDS Benefit at the Whitney. I have a limousine coming at eight after picking up Athena and her mother. What I don't have is a man who loves me enough to put on a black tie without complaining, who can play amiable escort without sacrificing his identity—something Mark never could do. He felt like a gigolo, he said, if I asked him to attend a business function and just be charming.

The entire industry will be there tonight, the ideal ambience for spreading the word about Athena. News travels fast. *Women's Wear Daily* called today to see what Athena would be wearing. A reporter from the "Eleven O'Clock News" asked for advance details on the Revlon deal and whether Athena was really born in Greece. I was tempted to say she was Ari Onassis's love child, but they might have believed me.

I'm close to tears because I have nobody to laugh with over the idiocies of my chosen profession. I'm close to tears because I was foolish enough, stupidly naive enough, to think maybe, just maybe, the man in Central Park would fill the breach. *Once more into his breeches, dear friend.*

Inside this steel-trap brain is a soap opera mentality forever spinning a breathless scenario: The handsome stranger would have been waiting for me this morning at the reservoir with razor nicks to indicate his anxiety. We would have run in tandem, silently celebrating our reunion. He would then have revealed he was a childless widower who never thought he could love again. And when I asked him to be my escort at tonight's benefit, he would have said he'd be honored and would've asked what time should he show up and where.

Missed chances twist my gut. I am in mourning for the lost moment. *For all sad words of tongue and pen, the saddest are these, "It might have been."* Corny, but true. I wouldn't dare quote Whittier out loud these days, but I often think of my high school English teacher, who urged us to remember Whittier and never allow happiness to slip away by default.

I am obsessed with what went wrong. I have rolled back the tape and played it again and again in slow motion to find the exact moment when a failure of nerve held me in check and let him disappear.

The truth is I still dance to an old, romantic tune. I wanted the tall, handsome stranger to pursue me and win my favor. In this high-tech, high-stakes state-of-the-art world, I may have succeeded in turning myself into a woman of steel. But I still have a marshmallow heart.

Maggie

Why is it so hard for me to talk to Dan? We're married sixteen years, and I still feel shy about discussing certain things. Personal things, I mean. Like he's been acting funny the last few months. Nothing I can put my finger on. Not depressed or anything serious, like the time he got back from Atlanta and I had to worm it out of him that he had had a bad scare at the hotel. He'd thought he was having a heart attack and called the hotel doctor. It turned out to be gastritis from too much southern hospitality. Even then I wouldn't have had a clue if I hadn't been doing the checkbook and asked him who was Dr. Forester.

Maybe it's mid-life crisis. If you don't have it, you can get it from reading about it in magazines. I wish I could get him to relax more. Maybe jogging is the answer after all. I try to make our home an oasis of calm. Maybe there's trouble at the office that he hasn't told me about. How he can be partners with that barracuda I'll never understand.

But it can't be money that's bothering him. This morning he urged me to go out and buy a new wardrobe for myself and the girls. Tonight, Jennifer is taking Sandi to a kids' concert at Lincoln Center. It'll be just Dan and me at dinner. I'm going to insist we talk. Maybe it's my fault.

Jennifer is so funny. She "happened" to leave a magazine open on my bed, showing a whole slew of Victoria's Secret lingerie. Is she trying to tell me something, the little minx?

Daniel

I'm feeling old and confused. My daughter has turned into Lolita. Yesterday she was my little girl. Now, if I didn't know she was only thirteen, I'd swear to God she was flirting with me, trying to turn me on. Parading around in her underwear. Making seductive cracks about sex. It's embarrassing. The other day she asked me if I thought sperm was fattening and whether I knew its caloric content—looking me straight in the eye. I didn't know which way to look. I could feel my ears getting hot, but I kept a straight face and said I didn't know for sure and to ask her mother.

This morning, she whispered that she was taking Sandi to a children's concert at Lincoln Center, leaving Maggie and me alone for a romantic dinner. "Please wear a condom, Dad. Two children is enough!"

I sense a conspiracy here. Maggie, who's never let the girls go anywhere at night by themselves, says that Jennifer's old enough for the responsibility. Lincoln Center is only five minutes away. They have instructions to take a cab home. "Won't it be nice for a change, just the two of us? We haven't had a chance to talk for ages, have we?"

I can't explain why, but I don't want a quiet dinner for two with Maggie. I've got a lot on my mind, but I just don't want to talk about it, any of it. Maybe it is mid-life crisis, a general malaise, dissatisfaction with everything. The agency's going great, this year almost double last year, so why isn't it enough? Why am I biting everyone's head off? I used to be Lovable Dan, now the staff cringes when I walk in. And Sonia is still acting like the Empress of China, like I'm her employee instead of her partner. She gets crazy when I hint at her retirement; she won't even discuss it.

Knowing Maggie, she'll haul out the candles and the flowers tonight. I can't deal with it. I know I have everything in life to make me happy, but I'm not. It's not Maggie's fault. I'm uneasy about being alone with her at the dinner table without the children to distract us. I don't know what to say to her.

And if I'm being honest, I keep thinking of that girl in yellow in Central Park, as if she, too, is part of what's missing in my life.

When I phoned home from the office, I pretended ignorance of the romantic dinner plans. "I've invited Sonia to join us.

She's always asking about you and the girls. After all, she is my business partner. We haven't had her over for ages."

I could hear Maggie's angry intake of breath. All she said was, "Fine. I hope she likes bluefish." (Since starting my new health kick, I've been cutting down on meat.)

She'd given in without a word, so why was I so mad? Why is she so docile, why didn't she put her foot down and say, "No. I'm sorry. Tell Sonia I've made other plans. Ask her to come next Tuesday when the girls will be here!" I want to shake her for letting me push her around.

Sonia

Something's going on. Maggie The Pill made me feel about as welcome as a boil on the behind. There were candles on the table. When I volunteered to light them, she said, "Don't bother. Dan hates candlelight."

Dan tried to smooth things over by lighting the candles himself. "It's just that I like to see the two most important women in my life."

"Does Sonia know you're out jogging every morning?" Maggie was trying to be the gracious hostess, but she sounded like she was accusing him of a crime.

"I don't tell Sonia everything, darling. After all, some things are sacred—like jogging." The man's trying, I thought.

"Everyone knows middle-aged men go jogging to meet young girls." Maggie has no talent for teasing.

"I asked you to run with me, didn't I? There are plenty of middle-aged women out there running their buns off."

"I am *not* middle-aged!" she flared. Surprised by the vehemence of her outburst, she tried to turn it into a joke, which clearly it was not.

She sure doesn't look middle-aged, whatever that means. These days, women are young forever, until one day their faces collapse into a wrinkled prune. Maggie's one of the lucky ones, the Good Bone people—slender, with strong facial structure, they look great till they're ninety—the bitch. So what's eating her? She's got a life millions of women would envy, a successful husband, a comfortable home, two kids who aren't dealing drugs or peddling their asses or robbing banks. If last night's little performance is a sample of how she's been acting, no wonder Dan insisted on bringing me home for dinner. He doesn't want to be alone with her.

Dammit, I hope this doesn't mean divorce. That's all I need—a partner in turmoil. He's one hell of a salesman, but I've seen personal problems drive other men down the toilet. I've got too much invested in Dan to let anything happen. If and when I do retire, I want to be sure of my income.

I wonder if he's got a little tootsie-roll on the side. Maybe that's what's eating her. I feel about Dan the way I felt about my husband: whatever he does is okay with me, as long as it doesn't affect the business.

Daniel

I insisted on taking Sonia downstairs to find a cab. Not that I was afraid she'd be mugged—God help any mugger who attacked Sonia; she'd tear his head off. But I had to get away from Maggie for a minute. She looked so hurt, I was afraid I'd make things worse by losing my temper.

"Sorry Maggie wasn't herself tonight," I said. "Forget it," Sonia said, adding the suggestion that maybe Maggie needed a change of scenery, a vacation somewhere by herself to "give you both a little space to move around in."

Instead of going back upstairs, I walked over to the all-night newsstand to pick up a magazine. Dinner or no dinner, I was suddenly ravenous with a nervous hunger. There's a twenty-four-hour Papaya joint on Broadway and Seventy-second Street. I had two hot dogs with sauerkraut and mustard and a large papaya-orange drink while I leafed through every page in the magazine. It could have been upside down or in Chinese for all I know. I couldn't concentrate on the stories, and I didn't want to go home.

By the time I got back, the girls were asleep and so was Maggie—or at lease she was pretending to be. As I lay beside her, wide awake, I began to think about that morning. How long had it been, two weeks since the girl in yellow? Who was I kidding? I knew exactly how long—thirteen days. Running on Riverside Drive was for the birds—too many cars, fumes, pollution. The Central Park reservoir was obviously superior. I felt foolish as hell, allowing a small, passing moment to affect me like this. What was so frightening about seeing some girl for all of six seconds? Why had it sent me hightailing to Riverside Drive like I was running for my life?

I suddenly remembered a moment in *Citizen Kane,* the part where Everett Sloane recalls seeing a girl on a ferryboat, never speaking to her or seeing her again, but confessing a lifetime of years later that a day had never gone by without thinking about her.

America's a free country, right? If I choose to jog around the Central Park reservoir, it's up to me, right? What am I afraid of?

A girl in a yellow sweat suit? Ridiculous. Anyway, it's a million-to-one shot that I'll ever run into her again.

Maggie

I feel shrink-wrapped, suffocating. I hate that woman; he knows it. She doesn't care beans about me or the girls or anything but Dan and the business he brings into the agency. He refuses to discuss her, it's strictly off limits. Even last summer, when the bookkeeper was sick and I went in to do the invoices and pay some bills and I found Sonia was charging her clothes to the company, Dan said forget it, it was none of my business.

His business is my business. Who does she think she is, Leona Helmsley? A two-thousand-dollar suede coat is not a business expense. I wanted to point out that the IRS wouldn't think so either, and that if there were an audit, they'd be in trouble. But I didn't have the guts to say any more. I'm afraid of fights. Dan and I have never really had a fight. I don't know how to fight. There's no point. I know I'd lose. I'd rather just give in and have peace.

When he took Sonia downstairs, I was relieved. It gave me a minute to collect myself. Looking out of the window, I saw him put her in a cab and wondered what I should say when he came back upstairs, or whether I should just be in the kitchen, straightening up and pretending everything was fine. When I saw him walk down the street, I realized he didn't want to face me either. By the time he got back, I was in bed reading. When I heard his key, I switched off the light and pretended to be asleep.

Something's really bothering him. He lay beside me like an iron statue, all rigid and cold. I longed to touch him, to reach out and hold him—not in a sexual way, only to comfort him and ask him what's wrong. But I was afraid—afraid he would shrug me away, and afraid that what was wrong was me.

Liza

Well, it finally happened. I'm hysterical. Call if kismet, call it anything you want. I'd totally forgotten the whole incident, totally put him out of mind. I had plenty of other things to think about—like Athena and her mother, and the set of Eurasian twins I had found at a high school beauty pageant and was transforming into supermodels, and a million and one other things, like making time for the dentist and my mother—when suddenly, there he was.

What's more, I was wearing my yellows. I must have a dozen sets of sweats in a veritable riot of colors. What I do is wear them in turn and wash them all at once. This morning, I realized the yellows were frayed and faded beyond chic and had a bad case of Les Droops, and I was about to rip them into dust rags when I decided no, I'd wear them one more time—and suddenly, there he was.

When I said "Hi!" he bolted like he'd been shot, picking up speed and disappearing in the clutch of joggers rounding a turn, his ears a rich burgundy. Bingo, bulls-eye—the dude remembered. He was running scared—hosannah! I felt totally, but totally, in control; like at that certain moment in a negotiation when you know it's okay. I didn't hang around. I didn't gallop after him or change direction in order to confront him head-on at the far side of the reservoir.

The fish was hooked. He'd be back tomorrow. I could wait. Today, I was the warrior queen with a potential battle on my hands. *New York* magazine was doing a cover story on hot new models, including Athena. Eileen Ford and Johnny Casablancas would be at the session with their new girls. Just because I had a contract with Athena didn't mean she couldn't be lured away. Contracts were made to be broken.

On my way to the office, I stopped off at Herman's for a new set of yellow sweats. I was still tingling with anticipation of the challenges that lay ahead when I got off the elevator and found Myrna holding the phone away from her ear while the other lines were lit up like a Christmas tree.

"She's got to speak to you. Urgently. Refuses to leave a message. Her name's Rosalind."

"Mother?" Why can't she admit she's my mother? She likes me to call her Rosalind; so okay, I call her Rosalind. I've asked her not to call me at the office, because I can't talk with her at the office, because too much is going on, and then she gets insulted because I put her on hold. Unless it's an emergency.

"Is it Daddy? What's wrong?" I have visions of rushing to the hospital and missing the *New York* session and losing Athena to Eileen Ford.

"Nothing's wrong. Everything's right." She had run into Mark. "He still loves you, Liza."

"You didn't just run into him. You called him, right?"

"What's the difference? Listen to me, I spoke to him. He isn't going to marry that Tiffany. He still loves you, Liza. He wants another chance—"

I wanted to kill her with my bare hands. Instead, I explained about Athena and *New York* magazine and told her she should be proud of me and that I would speak to her later. A month ago, I might have been interested in hearing about Mark and his undying love for me. Not today. Today I was planning to fall in love again, tomorrow morning in Central Park.

Daniel

I tried to apologize to Maggie for bringing Sonia home. She managed to avoid me. She was in the shower when I woke up and pushed past me when I said good morning. She spoke to me indirectly, through the girls: "Jennifer, tell your father to pick up some skim milk on his way back from jogging, that is if he wants milk in his coffee." "Sandi, ask Daddy if he wants his orange juice before or after jogging."

The way she kept saying "jogging," it sounded like some kind of filthy habit. As a matter of fact, I wasn't feeling all that great. I'd been awake half the night. I wasn't sure if it was the dinner fiasco or those hot dogs, or this enemy camp surrounding me—Maggie giving me the business; Jennifer repeating her mother's interoffice memo in icy tones and then refusing to kiss me; Sandi following her big sister's lead, though she didn't seem sure why.

This was one morning I would skip jogging entirely. My head was jogging enough. I took an aspirin and was in the bedroom trying to pick out a tie when Maggie said, "Have you given up jogging?" Perfect wife that she is, she'd laid a clean pair of sweatpants and sweatshirt across the bedroom chair.

So you can see that what happened this morning was all Maggie's fault. If she hadn't been needling me, I'd have dressed and gone straight to work. As it was, I really didn't expect to see the girl in yellow. Fantasies are one thing. I had thought about her and what I would say if I ever saw her again. As a matter of fact, I had mentioned the incident to a client over a business lunch. We'd gotten chummy; we're both married, both about the same age. He was telling me about a girl he knew in Philadelphia and how at first he was shit-scared it was going to wreck his life, but it hadn't and they had quality time together and nobody was getting hurt and he was a better husband and father because of it.

As to my girl in yellow, his advice was if I ever saw her again, "Go for it."

Easier said than done. The sun must have been blinding me, because I didn't see her until suddenly there she was, smiling and saying "Hi." I was so startled, I kept on going. She must think I'm a looney bird. One thing's for sure. She remembered me, and she'll be there tomorrow morning.

Maggie

The minute Dan got back from the park, I apologized for my behavior last night and this morning. There was no excuse for acting the way I did. It's just that I want him to be his own man, to be in business for himself, and I hate seeing Sonia take advantage of him.

"You're right, you're absolutely right, and you are especially right about her charging clothes to the business. I'm going to add up all her personal expenses, and you, my darling Maggie, are going on a shopping spree of your own, anything you want, to even things up!"

What got into him? I wondered. Jogging certainly agreed with him. He was a different man from the one who'd left the house an hour before—buoyant, affectionate, singing while he dressed.

"Dan—" For weeks now I'd been thinking about getting a job. This seemed like a good time to ask what he thought.

"Would you tie my tie for me, Angel?" He knows I like tieing his tie, and it makes me blush when he calls me Angel.

"Dan—there's something I wanted to discuss—"

"I'm running late. Is it something we can talk about fast?"

He knows how long-winded I can get when I discuss things. The job idea could wait. I didn't want to lose the intimacy of the moment. "I was just thinking—jogging is doing you so much good, I might go with you tomorrow."

The bubble burst. He looked instantly deflated. Was it me? *Now* what had I done? Was it a crime to change my mind? Something was bothering him, something serious. I could see that now. Why couldn't he talk to me? Dammit, I'm his wife.

"Maggie, *please*—" He was brushing me off like a pesky mosquito.

"Maggie, please what? *What?* What did I say that's so terrible? You said it yourself, right in front of Sonia. You said you asked me to go jogging with you, and now that I want to go, you've changed your mind. What's wrong? Are you afraid I can't keep up? Are you still mad at me for saying you're too old?"

He flushed and refused to meet my eyes. "We'll discuss it later. Got to go."

"All I asked you is a simple question. I deserve a simple answer. Why don't you want me to go jogging with you?"

"You don't understand."

He looked trapped. It scared me. What had I done? Why was my husband itching to get away from me?

"You're right, Daniel. I don't understand."

Deception has never come easy to him. Now he was clearly groping for a palatable excuse for his behavior.

"Please, Maggie, bear with me. You know the stress I'm under. Surrounded by people day and night, at the office, at home, Sonia, clients, staff, the girls, you—"

"*Me*—but I'm your wife!"

He was instantly contrite. "I knew it. I knew you'd be hurt. Please, Maggie, think about it from my point of view. I'm never alone. It's nobody's fault, it's the way things are. You have time for yourself during the day, don't you? Well, consider the fact that I don't. I didn't realize how much I needed a little time out until I started jogging. I hate you to feel left out, darling, but it's what I need, to be alone in the fresh air and let my mind roll on. You do understand, don't you?"

I don't. I feel left out; and Daniel's right, I do feel hurt, deeply hurt, that my husband doesn't want me to go with him. I am also scared, because something is happening that has not happened before. He wants me to understand, but I don't understand and I'm scared.

Liza

His name is Dan. He's in the travel business. His office is on Third Avenue near Bloomingdale's, not far from me. It didn't take long to find out that, yes, he's married and the father of two girls, Jennifer and Sandi. I didn't ask his wife's name. They live in one of those old West Side apartments near the Dakota, where John Lennon was shot and Yoko still lives with Sean.

What did I expect, a man with no previous history or current connections? A match made in heaven? It could have been the case, I tell myself. Stranger things have happened. He could be a widower or divorced from a woman who ran away with a ski instructor, or a bachelor scientist married to his work for years but now ready for marriage and a family. None of the above, dammit. Face it, the man is married. Period.

Still, it was wonderful to flop down on the grass in the sweet morning air with the Manhattan skyline in the distance. I didn't mention yesterday morning or ask him why he ran like a frightened deer (I know I do that to men). He was so genuinely nice, a little shy at first, not one of those married hit men. We talked nonstop like old friends, finishing each other's sentences, laughing just to laugh, until I was startled to see I would be late for my first meeting.

"Will I see you tomorrow?" he asked with a smile so sweet I could feel my heart stop.

I shrugged. "Maybe yes and maybe—" I was a good fifty yards away, heading east toward Fifth Avenue and feeling his smile on my back, before I turned and shouted "—yes!"

Daniel

I can't stop thinking about her. I'm walking around in a daze like a lovesick kid. "My name is Liza with a Z, just like Liza Minnelli," she said. She's a talent agent with her own shop, handling mostly models and actors, newcomers she's building into superstars, like this discovery of hers, Athena. I have to admit this is new territory for me. I haven't heard of half the people she mentioned except in the gossip columns. "I'm very successful," she informed me with a sort of toughness that only accentuated her softness and vulnerability, like a belligerent kitten.

"My daughter wants to be a model," I said. "She's only thirteen, and I know I sound prejudiced because she's my kid, but believe me, she could be the next Brooke Shields. *Prettier* than Brooke Shields." Proud Poppa popping his buttons.

"Well, she has a handsome father, doesn't she? So she must be pretty. Send her to see me. I'll sign her up!" Flattery will definitely get you somewhere. I did not think it appropriate to say the mother is good-looking, too, and was in fact a model before she got married.

Maggie hasn't mentioned jogging with me again, though she manages to let me know she feels hurt. Or is it just my imagination? Liza has cast a spell over me. It's strange to feel so intimately connected to someone I've only known a few weeks. All we've done is run around the reservoir and hang out together on the grass, talking about everything under the sun. I haven't even held her hand, but I feel so guilty about wanting to that I can hardly look Maggie in the eye.

Being with Liza has made me realize there's something important missing in my marriage. I feel so comfortable with Liza, so energized, so alert, so ready to have opinions and laugh at silly things. I feel so confused. I'm not betraying Maggie. I don't even know Liza's last name or where she lives, apart from it being east of the park. She hasn't offered more and I haven't asked, as if each of us is waiting for the other to make the next move. I don't know what I want to happen next. What I do know is I can't wait to see her.

Tonight, Maggie has served a family favorite, pasta primavera. She's going across the street to a neighborhood beautification meeting while I help the girls with their homework. She has gaily promised to bring us back some ice cream if we promise to be good. The girls solemnly promise to be good. The minute she's gone, they squeal with excitement and attack me with hugs and tickles until I insist we cut out the horseplay and get down to business. "Or else, no ice cream!"

No one who has never experienced it can every truly appreciate the proprietary surge of joy, the savage pride a father takes in his children's accomplishments. I read Jennifer's essay on *Ivanhoe* and foresee a brilliant academic future, a master's degree in literature, a Rhodes scholarship. I correct Sandi's single mistake in arithmetic and blame the ambiguity of her textbook for leading her to the wrong conclusion.

These are my babies—so pretty, so smart, so greedy for life, so needy of me and all I can give them. I am the paterfamilias swaggering with satisfaction in the rewards of my domestic world. Yet I am also anticipating tomorrow and wondering with the sharp excitement of an adolescent boy what will happen in Central Park when I see Liza.

Liza

I couldn't stand it another minute. This morning when we finished running, my neck and shoulders went into spasm, as if my head was in a vise that was getting tighter and tighter. Stress was taking its toll; I was tied up in knots, the down side of being a killer shark. I couldn't move my head.

"Let me," he said. Standing close behind me, his breath on my neck, his hands found the hidden places as if he had eyes in his fingertips, his thumbs pressing the angry knots into jelly. My neck and shoulders surrendered themselves to his ministrations, graceful and flexible in response to a trustworthy lover. The world around us disappeared, the runners, the reservoir, the trees, all but the grassy ridge on which we stood. I thought I would die on the spot of erotic arrest. Some skin responds to other skin; call it *skinbiosis.* I couldn't stand it another minute.

"Let's have coffee at my place." My excuse was that I was expecting an important call from London before my office opened.

He knew and I knew that he knew it was a ruse to get him home. It's been weeks (it feels like years!) since we first fell into the morning routine of running around the reservoir and then stopping for coffee at one of those outdoor snack bars with the green and white umbrellas.

It's obvious and a little bit touching to see he's not in the habit of cheating. He's never even asked, "Do you live alone?" That, I discovered since getting back into circulation after my divorce, is the tip-off question of the married man on the prowl who hates to waste his precious time on someone with a roommate.

At first I had assured myself the situation was totally safe, pleasant, and contained, limited to a companionable workout followed by some friendly conversation while we cooled down. Except I was not cooling down and neither was he.

For days and days, I had been hoping he would make the move. Instead, day after day after *day,* we would reach the moment of murmuring it was getting late and head across Central Park in opposite directions. Clearly, it was up to me. He looked stunned at my suggestion but also relieved, as if to say "at last." I guess there's a little less guilt for him if I play the role of seducer.

We ran in unison, not saying a word, all the way to my apartment. As the elevator rose to my floor, the tension was unbearable. We could not look at each other. The keys trembled in my hand. He finally had to take them from me and open the door.

Daniel

Gentle is the word, astonishingly gentle. Wild, crazy, laughing, shrieking, crashing around on the floor, pulling off our clothes, knocking over lamps; but gentle all the same, the floor hard and soft—thick carpet, cool bare wood. The floor is for loving, an indoor meadow, a beach without sand, better than beds. Maggie refused to make love on the floor even in the early days before the children. She said married couples made love in bed. I only thought of Maggie fleetingly and much later on my way home, wondering if she would notice anything.

I was shit-scared by the time we got to Liza's. What in hell was I doing? She was nervous, too, so nervous she couldn't get her door open. When she gave me the key, she said, "You're the man. Put it in!" The bitch, I nearly tore the door off its hinges—but I was terrified. After so much stress, so much waiting and hoping and wanting her and not knowing what to do next, here I was in her apartment, afraid I might disgrace myself, afraid of all the things you read about and hear about and see on TV—going limp, not being able to get it up and keep it up, being too small to satisfy her, coming too soon, all the jokes about premature ejaculation.

I wanted so desperately to excite her, to know how to touch her and kiss her and turn her on. I felt so inadequate, so lacking in technique, a pathetic square, a nerd. What did I know about fancy fucking? Liza moved in sophisticated circles, what would she expect of me, this jerk she brought home, this idiot who didn't know what to do? She led the way without seeming to. Or did she? Or was the erotic instinct there all the time waiting to be aroused, guiding me with breathless certainty to caress her thighs and kiss her belly and stroke her breasts and eyelids and try to be everywhere and touch everywhere and do everything at once and make her moan and call my name?

I suddenly realized I was a young lover for the first time in my life—joyful, passionate, and as in control of my body as a dancer. I had never been a young lover. I had been younger and I had scored, banged, made out, fucked, got in—but never as a lover, never like this. There'd been a lot of women before Maggie, a lot of one-night stands and recreational sex. The sex revolution had been in high gear, women had the pill, the diaphragm, and the right to orgasm. Things were supposed to improve between men and women. The early days of any revolution are chaotic.

I respected women, or at least I thought I did. I didn't call them chicks or birdbrains like some men did. Before I met Maggie, I was running around with Stacey, a jewelry designer in Greenwich Village. Talk about failure of communication; I assumed because we were sleeping together that we'd be getting married. Her life-style got wilder and wilder—drugs, sex with other men, with other women, Eastern religions, fasting. I couldn't keep up. I thought it was a phase. When I brought her an engagement ring, she sneered at me. "You don't want a woman, you want a mother! Wipe your own ass, wash your own socks, you make me vomit."

Had I insulted her by asking her to marry me? Why was she so angry?

"All women are angry. We've sublimated for so long, we don't know why we're so angry—we have to find out."

Several months later, I felt compelled to tell her about meeting Maggie and that we were going to be married. Maggie, I explained, was the perfect woman for me—serene, dignified, pretty, intelligent, devoted, and not the least bit angry.

"That's what you think!"

Stacey couldn't stay away from me entirely. It wasn't so much me personally that she wanted, it was the excitement. She invited me to a bachelor lunch the day before my wedding and took me back to her loft for "old times' sake." She had an uncanny way of showing up at Clarke's where I usually drank beer. The day after Jennifer was born, I fell into my own postpartum depression, feeling lonely and left out and ashamed of my jealous rage when the newborn clamped her mouth on Maggie's nipple and nestled against the breasts where I wanted to find comfort after all the stress of the pregnancy and the birth itself.

With the unerring instinct of a bird of prey, Stacey found me and took me once again to her feathered nest. This betrayal of my wife, my marriage, my new daughter, really made me sick. Stacey phoned or showed up from time to time, but I never had anything more to do with her. "Like I said," she reminded me sarcastically, "You don't want a woman, you want a mother."

She was probably right. I had the mother of my children at home and I had Sonia ever-present, ever-watchful at the office. I couldn't pull anything even if I wanted to, and until I met Liza, I hadn't wanted to or really had the opportunity. Last year, Sonia had hired a new receptionist, a sensational-looking kid straight out of Katie Gibbs. At the office Christmas party, she kissed me like she meant it and wiggled her finger in my ear, an effort observed by Sonia, who didn't mention it to me but made the youngster's life so miserable she quit.

I've listened to men talk about their conquests and smiled knowingly. Some men were oblivious to the women's movement. They still talk about bimbos and pulling birds and the little stewardess or little actress who can't resist them. In my business it's important to be one of the boys and share the camaraderie of their sexual triumphs, however exaggerated.

Lying on Liza's floor, wrapped in Liza's arms, passion spent, I vow that whatever happens, I will never discuss her with anyone. What has happened here this morning is precious and personal. There are pillows behind our heads. A calico quilt has materialized from somewhere and covers our naked bodies, now tranquil after the storm.

I don't want to move. I want to stay this way forever. My face is against her neck. I kiss her throat and taste salt. It's then that I realize I am crying.

Liza

See a man and pick him up
All the day you'll have good luck.
Let a lover get away
You'll be sorry all the day.

Such sweetness. The man trembled like a leaf. He's over forty, but suddenly his face shone with the eager shyness of the inexperienced, like the young men in classic French novels who fall into the clutches of Marguerite Gautier and Fanny Legrand. There was something about him that made me feel wildly sophisticated, a woman with a past who knew all the tricks and could teach him one or two.

When he finally got the key into the lock, I gasped, "Dan, you found the G-Spot," just to tease; and I was about to ask how he wanted his coffee, when he had me down on the floor in the doorway, kissing me and hugging me and trying to smile into my eyes and tearing off my sweats and calling my name and shouting "Wow!" all at the same time; and me helping and trying to get us inside the apartment so I could slam the door so that the door man wouldn't find us on the welcome mat when he delivered the mail.

I've forgotten how many square inches of skin cover the human body. Every pore, every follicle tensed with expectation; my entire sex alarm system activated, and his slightest grazing touch set off siren shrieks like a smoke detector in a tiny kitchen.

What would we do without song titles? It's been a long, long time since I've felt this way and been able to respond like this. You can plan the opportunity, but you can't plan the chemistry between two people. There has to be spontaneous combustion.

Since Mark, I've put myself quite literally into the hands of skilled practitioners of sex. These are the men women whisper about and recommend to one another like hairdressers, the Macho Mechanics. Women pretend to like the idea of these men who "really like women" and whose stated mission in life is to "make women happy." They are so knowledgeable about the female anatomy and how it functions they could be surgeons. The Macho Mechanic is not a gigolo. He is usually successful, if not rich rich. His hobby is giving women orgasms. Some men collect stamps or pipes or baseball cards. The Macho Mechanic prides himself on his efficiency and seems—dispassionately—to take quiet pleasure in a job well done.

The concept was intriguing for a while and certainly took me through the divorce with what I chose to believe was well-deserved gratification in my time of emotional need; and it was preferable to eating and putting on weight. I couldn't really complain about being used, since I was being served—or serviced—with as much sexual joy as my poor, out-of-shape thirty-year-old body could stand. That's when I switched to jogging.

Dan was awkward, he was fumbling, he nearly cracked my head open on the coffee table. He managed to rip a seam in my sweat pants, and I wound up with one sneaker on my otherwise naked body because he couldn't untie the laces. He was also touchingly ardent in the way he made love, the ways he tried to excite me, listening with his entire body for my response. Thank God he didn't ask me if it was good for me. I wish men would stop asking that; I'd like to stomp on whoever thought it up in the first place! The truth is, when it's right, it's right. It didn't matter much what he did or I did, it was right for both of us; and soom we were crocheted together in our own intricate pattern.

The agony was getting up. The agony was disentangling ourselves and trying to talk in a matter-of-fact way about how late it was and how we both better get a move on. I went into the kitchen so he could use the phone in private. I eavesdropped, of course, as he told his wife he had met a client in the park and was about to hop a cab home.

Before he left, he solemnly told me I had made him the happiest man in the world, and could he borrow five dollars for a cab? I nearly made a joke about five dollars being cheap for his incredible performance, but I bit my tongue just in time.

In the pounding hot shower, I scrubbed with a loofah and did a frame-by-frame replay of the morning's scenario, stopping at the good parts and running them again. More than anything, my body wanted sleep, wanted to stretch out in cool sheets under the calico quilt in my darkened bedroom and dream the rest of the day away.

Marguerite Gautier would have done just that, but we know what happened to her. Destiny was calling with the voice of my secretary. Eileen Ford wasn't lolling in bed, was she? If I wanted my piece of the pie, I'd better get moving.

A few hours later, I had just finished my twentieth conversation of the day with Athena's mother and was about to hire a hit squad to take her out when Myrna buzzed in great excitement to announce, "Flowers. A ton of them!"

Tucked into the long-stem yellow roses was an envelope containing a crisp new five-dollar bill. The note said, "Have dinner with me tomorrow night."

Maggie

I've never seen him act this way, almost rude. All I said was that I was beginning to worry when he didn't get back that maybe he'd been mugged or gotten hit by a car.

"Give me a break, Maggie. I told you, I ran into a client, we had some coffee, and the time flew by."

"I was so worried, I was about to call the police."

"Stop keeping tabs on me. So I was a few minutes late."

"Two hours is not two minutes. You're in the park in your running clothes with no identification, right? Anything might have happened. You could have had a heart attack. Who'd have known who you are?"

"You keep harping about heart attacks, heart attacks. I am

not an old man, I am in good physical condition, and exercise is going to keep me that way."

Why couldn't he see how upset I was, my imagination running overtime, looking out the window, watching for him? When I tried to explain, tried to make him understand how petrified I had been, how at one point I saw an ambulance racing into the park and thought what if it's my husband—do you know what my husband did? Something he's never done in nearly fifteen years of marriage: he told me to shut up.

Then I started to pick up his sweats to put them in the washing machine.

"Stop waiting on me, Maggie. I can put them in the machine."

Something's bothering him, but as usual, he doesn't want to talk about it. As usual, I'm in the dark. Is it Sonia? The office? He refuses to talk about money; I have no idea if business is good or bad. Are we rich, are we broke? I've stopped asking him about the details of his partnership with Sonia. We have two children, dammit. What would happen if he did have a heart attack? Would Sonia send me a designer wreath from Bergdorf's?

I used to feel so safe, so protected. "Just leave everything to me, Maggie. You take care of the home and kids. I'll take care of bringing home the bacon." It was so cozy. I felt so cherished. I was one of the lucky ones, a romantic heroine with a big strong handsome husband and a happily-ever-after marriage like an old Doris Day movie.

More and more, I see how I've conspired to create my own ignorance. "What you don't know can't hurt you"—whoever said that should have his tongue cut out. I've closed my eyes and shut my ears to the harsh realities for too long, deluding myself, telling myself that's what Daniel wanted, the perfect submissive wife. A few years back, he told me about his will and about his insurance policies and the provisions he has made in case something happens. He went over the details with me, but the thought of losing him was so upsetting, I can't remember a thing. I keep telling myself that life is real, life is earnest, and I could wake up tomorrow and find myself alone with the children.

The hum of the washing machine soothes me. I like watching the clothes dry. I often wonder what it would be like to be whirled around like that and come out all warm and fluffy. I still like touching Dan's things, smoothing them out, folding them up, putting them away. I wonder what happened to his running socks? I know he was wearing the purple ones when he went to the park. I watched him put them on. They're not in the washing machine. Maybe he didn't throw them in. Maybe he kicked them under the bed.

The girls are at school. The house is spotless. I guess I'm feeling sorry for myself, a case of the ab-dabs. Nobody needs me anymore. I could disappear tomorrow and nobody would notice.

I've turned on "All My Children," but I've lost track of the various story lines. Their lives are so complicated. Mine is almost nonexistent. I've been tempted to phone in to Dr. Ruth or Sonya Freedman or Oprah or Phil, but the problem is—what's my problem?

I've got everything I ever dreamt of having except for a career, but who needs a career when you've got everything else? The last time I mentioned going back to work, Daniel said we didn't need the money, that the girls and he needed me at home, but that the decision was mine to make.

You see, Dr. Ruth, I've decided to go back to work, but I'm afraid to tell my husband.

Myrna

Working for Liza is really awesome. It's been over a month since I got out of film school and answered her ad for a personal assistant. It's not film, of course, but it's very exciting—fielding phone calls, coordinating details, working with the models and the ad agencies. It's really neat.

Liza is the coolest. She can deal with things that would blow your mind. Models showing up stoned, clients changing their mind. One day, somebody hijacked this delivery van with an entire week's film. A million-dollar shoot—gone! The troops fell apart. Did you ever see an Ad Row heavy cry like a baby? Awesome.

Everyone was going ape-shit, but not Liza. She put the whole thing back together—eight models, two stylists, all the clothes, the accessories, the photographer—and she even led a group prayer for sunshine. And when they all came back to the office with champagne and caviar to celebrate and thank her, all she said was, "No problem."

I didn't think anything could ever make her lose her cool, including Athena's mother, until today when those yellow roses arrived. I've never seen Liza like that; she started hyperventilating like she was going to pass out. She was *shaking* when she opened the note, and she picked up one of the roses with two fingers like it might break and raised it to her lips with this dreamy look in her eyes—and then she closed her eyes and kissed it. Then she noticed me standing there and told me to close her office door *on my way out* and hold all calls.

I'm dying to know who sent them. Clients send stuff all the time—bottles of wine, fancy cheese, cases of the products they represent. But this was no client gift. This was a guy. It's so romantic. How come I never meet anyone who sends flowers?

There goes the phone again. I know it's going to be Athena's mother again, asking for money.

Daniel

Every instinct tells me I'm asking for big trouble and to stop right now. Leave town. Grow a beard. Forget the whole thing. Cut bait before I get eaten alive. But how can I? And anyway, why should I? (Don't answer that question—I know damn well why I should.)

There's no way I can keep on seeing her. Not after yesterday. I'm a basket case. I've been dropping things. I bought a fifty-dollar tie. I shaved twice. I tipped a cabbie a ten instead of a single. This morning I left my briefcase home and had to go back and get it.

The children haven't noticed, but Maggie was more withdrawn than usual last night, the way she gets when something's bothering her. And I have to pry it out of her because she'll never volunteer to talk. It's one of the things that's always been wrong with our marriage. She's always shut me out of her innermost thoughts. Okay, so I'm not being fair, I'm looking for excuses to justify my behavior. I do love Maggie. She's a good wife and mother. But in a way she's an automaton, programmed to be cool, calm, collected, efficient, and totally predictable—like a computer system.

Last night I was worried she'd ask me what happened to my socks. In my rush to leave Liza's, I couldn't find them. That's why I snapped Maggie's head off and insisted on stuffing my sweats into the machine myself—that and because I was afraid there might be some sign of Liza on them. If she noticed about the socks, she hasn't said anything. If it comes up, I'll say I don't know what she's talking about. Ignorance is more convincing than an elaborate excuse like maybe a squirrel ate them.

Not funny. The situation is not funny at all. I should have my head handed to me, but I can't help myself. I want Liza. I can't wait to see her tonight. Not just for sex. There's so much more than that. Those wicked eyes, that laugh, the things she says. So funny, so warm, so giving. Even before yesterday, she sent some travel business my way, can you believe it? One of her fashion accounts was complaining about their travel agent, so she told them to call me. I have friends for twenty years who never think of recommending me to anyone.

She makes me feel like I can conquer the world. I noticed she wears silver jewelry. There was this Paloma Picasso ad in today's *Times.* I'm going to get her a little something as a surprise over dinner. I stopped thinking of surprises for Maggie a long time ago. She says they embarrass her or cost too much, and she usually insists on returning them.

Liza won't be embarrassed. Liza will be crazy about it. I can just see her face when she opens the package; that lively, inquisitive face, ready for anything. On second thought, I'll wait and give it to her after dinner, when we're alone. At her place.

Maggie

Something's wrong. It's in the air. Even the girls sense it. Sandi's been pestering me all afternoon, since the minute she got home from school: "When's Daddy coming home?" Time has a different meaning for an eight-year-old. She got an A-Plus on her European Geography project. My praise isn't enough. I'm just good old Mommy. She wants her father. Dan helped her with it. They had such a good time. He brought home all those travel folders and maps and things and now she wants him to pat her and hug her.

Jennifer is also driving me crazy. If she doesn't start menstruating soon, I'm going to flip my lid. Someone once called adolescence a disease. I hope we can live through the next few years; and then, of course, it'll be Sandi mooning around, draping herself on the furniture, parading around in her underwear and throwing herself into Dan's lap—but with one eye always on the nearest mirror, just like Jennifer.

"Be patient. Dad'll be home for dinner," I assured Sandi.

"No, he won't," Jennifer said in that sing-song, smarty-pants tone that can lead to murder.

"What do you mean? Did he call? Why didn't you tell me?"

"*Mom!* Lighten up!" The exasperated brat. I could really have slapped her face.

"Jennifer, if you knew how ugly you look when you twist your mouth like that, you'd stop doing it."

"I *know,* you've told me a million times, it'll *freeze* that way. But Daddy told me, this *morning,* before he went jogging, that he would probably be having a business dinner tonight and he would see me in the morning! *Comprende?*"

It was news to me. "The wife is the last to know" is a family joke, like when we run out of milk. Now I was starting to feel paranoid.

The phone rang. He was sorry to be calling so late, but a client was in town and he hadn't found out until a minute ago that they were having dinner.

"Why not bring him home?" I suggested. "Dinner's all cooked, the new Craig Claiborne bouillabaise. There's enough for an army."

It seemed the client wanted to try one of those new Thai places in Soho. "Sounds like fun," I said. Why didn't I join them? With both my daughters watching me like hawks scenting blood, I managed to trill my wifely understanding. Of course we'd do it another time. Of course I realized it was business, not social.

"See you later," I said, hoping the girls could not hear his "Don't wait up!"

What good would it do me if I did? He hasn't touched me in months.

Liza

At first I felt guilty. The man's married with two children; he's living at home. Then I decided it's not my problem, it's his problem; it's nothing to do with me. Now I've decided to stop worrying and live for today. Nothing is perfect. Nothing is forever. I thought I was happy once. A good marriage, I thought. A good husband. And then Mark admitted he was "not happy," that "something was missing," that I "expected too much." At thirty-two, it never occurred to me that my husband would leave me for a younger woman.

But it happened. I found them together in my bed. It still hurts. And now *I'm* the Other Woman. But it's different with Dan. I just want to spend a little time with him. I'll never ask him to leave his wife. And I'm not going to sit home on Saturday nights like the weekend widows I know. Thanks, but no thanks. I've promised myself to put him in a separate compartment and to continue meeting and dating other men until I find an eligible man who's ready for a relationship. It's been rough since Mark and I split, but they're out there and I intend to find one. My friend Alicia met a guy through a personal ad in *New York* magazine. She swore me to secrecy. I'm not that desperate. Yet.

The truth is I'm scared. I'm absolutely besotted with Dan. That first morning when we finally got it together, I was beside myself. Then I found his socks and my heart was in my mouth. What would he tell his wife? Then I told myself, what did I care what he told his wife? It was his problem, not mine. But my conscience was eating me alive. How could I do to another woman what was done to me? After that first crazy morning and that first crazy week, afternoons at my place instead of lunch, evenings at my place instead of dinner, I called a halt. "We've got to talk."

I was giddy, I was whacko, I was letting things slide at the office, ignoring messages, telling Myrna to say I was in a meeting, avoiding decisions and unpleasantness like Athena's mother because I was head over heels in love; or put another way, I was a stupid bitch in heat. Whatever the diagnosis, the whole thing was ridiculous and immoral. I told Dan it had to stop.

My mistake was telling him when we were alone, at my place, naked and in bed. He folded me in his arms and assured me that I wasn't taking anything away from his marriage. Maggie and he were like other old married couples. There was no bad feeling. They were civil to each other. Most marriages were like that after several years. I hadn't been married long enough to find that out, he reminded me. He and Maggie were devoted to the girls. He earned the money, she took care of the home. He wasn't cheating her of anything. He wasn't taking anything away from her to give to me.

I can't help myself. I'm so miserable without him, and so ecstatic when we meet, that I've decided to take each moment of happiness as it comes. You can't negotiate joy. Janis Joplin said to "get it while you can." I've dated other men since Mark. One turned out to be a coke head. Another thought I could help his career as a photographer. The most recent insisted on giving me the details of his incestuous relationship with his sister. I being so worldly, he knew I'd understand.

The good men, as has been noted, are taken or are in hiding and are therefore hard to find. Some, like Dan, are less taken than others. Oh, I know I'm just making excuses. It takes talent to rationalize guilt, and I am a very talented lady.

Last night, he stayed over for the first time. It was so wonderful to wake up, shower together, and argue about breakfast—whether oat bran muffins are edible or should be fed to the pigeons and who gets the first section of the *Times* first. I didn't ask how he managed it. He volunteered the information—he had told his wife he was in Chicago, where he was flying today. Being in the travel business has its rewards.

After he left for the airport, I noticed he left his toilet articles and robe in my bathroom, like he's moved in but he hasn't moved in. It makes me feel uneasy, sort of invaded, like who invited him to make himself at home. It scares me a little though I'm not exactly sure why. I'm glad I'm going to California next month. It'll give me a chance to think things through.

Maggie

Tonight, Daniel was home for dinner, for a change. Sandi refused to let him kiss her. "Hey, Punkin', what's wrong?" he asked. But he knew damn well what was wrong. It's the first time he's been home on time in over two weeks. In fact, he's hardly home for dinner at all anymore, and when he is, he's late or preoccupied. I hope nothing's wrong at the office or with his stomach. I'm afraid to ask if he's gone for a checkup. He's on such a short fuse lately, he'd probably bite my head off.

This morning, I said, "Anything wrong?"

"What could possibly be wrong? You're the perfect wife. The children are perfect. The house is perfect. The agency doubled last year's figures. So please stop bugging me. Nothing is wrong."

But there is something wrong and the girls notice it, too. Tonight, Sandi made a big production of setting the table just so, her sweet little forehead furrowed in concentration as she lined up the cutlery and folded the napkins in triangles—much too busy as Mother's little helper to give Daddy the time of day. I wanted to kiss her myself.

Jennifer was in her room getting ready for a birthday party across the hall. "Weird or Wonderful Costumes," the invitation had read. She had refused to let me help—"It's a surprise," she'd said. I couldn't wait to see her getup.

"Jennifer—dinner!" Sandi sang out as we sat down at the table.

"Well? Where the hell is she?" Dan knows very well I don't like that kind of language in front of the children. They hear enough vulgarity on the outside. I tell Sandi to knock on the door.

"She's all in a state of nerves, Dan. She's going to a costume party."

"At night? She's only thirteen."

"Across the hall. She's all excited. Tell her she looks beautiful."

"That's no reason to keep the family waiting!"

Okay, so we're waiting. How long, ten seconds? Two minutes? Who was he to crack the whip? Just because he's decided to honor us with his presence is no reason to turn the house upside down. What's the big rush, anyway? And since when is he so concerned about the family?

"Maggie, I'm going to count to ten. If Jennifer isn't at this table by then, she's grounded. No party. No TV—"

Jennifer chose that moment to make her entrance. Beaming with excitement, her pubescent body a glittering assault on the senses, she clearly had no idea how sexy she looked. The black eye makeup, the exaggerated mouth, the slashed jeans that exposed her thighs, the bare midriff with lipsticked arrows pointing to her belly button. I didn't know whether to laugh or cry.

Dan blew his top. "How dare you walk around like that?"

Jennifer's face fell like a circus clown's. "But—"

He turned on me. "You're her mother!"

"It's a costume party. Rock and roll. Ring-Dings, nachos, Diet Coke—kid stuff—"

Jennifer had recovered her poise. "It's the punk look. I'm a punk rocker, don't you understand? Beth's father's got a Minicam. He's going to make a music video of the party and we're all going to get a copy."

"You're not stepping out of this house in that getup. You look like a Times Square whore."

How could he say such a thing? Tears streamed down the little-girl face behind the garish makeup. "Is that where you go every night, Daddy? Times Square?"

Jennifer ran sobbing to her room. Sandi climbed into my lap and began to suck her thumb, her head against my breast. *Baby, baby.*

Dan seemed stunned by the havoc he had caused. "Come on Sandi. You're too big to suck your thumb. You want to spoil your pretty smile? Come to Daddy, Punkin'." He tried gently to dislodge her thumb, causing her to shriek convulsively and cling to me for dear life. My husband's pained eyes met mine in bewilderment and accusation.

"You owe Jennifer an apology, Dan."

"She looks like a hooker."

"She looks like a thirteen-year-old going to a rock and roll party."

"If you say so. Do whatever you want. Let her go naked. Who cares what I say, I'm just her father, what do I know? I'm going out."

"But what about dinner?"

"I've lost my appetite."

"Where are you going?"

"A client."

Sandi piped up. "Why are you always meeting clients? Who needs clients? I hate clients. Why do you have to meet a client now?"

"Yes, Dan, tell Sandi why you have to meet a client now."

Dan's face was angrier than I've ever seen it. "Please remind your mother and sister that we have a pretty nice life-style. Somebody's got to pay for it. That's why I'm meeting a client!"

Daniel

I don't know what got into me, landing on Jennifer like that, the poor kid. It was probably just the shock of seeing her like that. Kids that age don't understand their sexuality. All done up like she was asking to be raped. When she got home, I asked if she'd had a good time at the party, but she won't talk to me. Neither will Sandi. She's the street fighter. I thought she was going to knock me flat on my keister.

It's not funny. I can't think straight. I've only known Liza for a little over a month, but it's like she's always been part of me. It's tearing me apart.

I can't stand this double life much longer. I can't stand deceiving Maggie like this, but I can't face telling her either. She knows something's going on. I keep waiting for her to accuse me, but she doesn't. It's driving me batty. She accepts every excuse, every lie. I say I'll be away overnight—she says fine. I say I'm taking a client to dinner and I may be late—she says have a good time.

She has cloaked herself in a steel shawl of serenity. If she has something to say, she says it quietly, without histrionics. Like Jennifer's outfit. "You owe Jennifer an apology, Dan." It was like she was saying "Please pass the salt." The more inconsiderate I am, the more considerate she is, so I really feel like a prize shit. The household runs like an oiled machine, my suits go to the cleaners, my shirts and underwear are perfect. She treats me like the lord and master—emotional warfare at its most insidious. It's like that old peace poster: What If They Gave a War and Nobody Came?

She refuses to fight. Whatever I say goes. I'm sure if I suggested building a campfire in the middle of the living room, she'd say that if that's what I wanted to do, it would be okay with her.

How can I tell her that I've fallen head over heels in love with another woman? That I didn't mean for it to happen, but I can't live without her? That I want a divorce?

"Maggie, I want a divorce." I can say it in the shower or walking along the street. I still haven't the guts to say it to her face. She's playing hardball, pretending not to notice. The girls looked so sad this morning. Jennifer knocked over her milk and blamed Sandi; Sandi just sat and refused to eat, her thumb in her mouth.

It kills me to see them upset, but Liza is part of me now, I can't give her up. I've asked myself a million times, what if I'd never met her? I'd be happy with my life, wouldn't I? But the fact is I *did* meet her, and I want to spend the rest of my life with her.

Poor Maggie, it's not her fault, she's the perfect wife. What can I say to her? Maybe I'll suggest a trial separation. After all, the woman has her pride. I'll discuss it with Liza. That's what so wonderful about her. I can tell her anything. I'm so happy with her. The chemistry is so perfect. I feel so absolutely at home in her apartment, like I belong there with her.

I feel so alienated from Maggie, like we're strangers. Maybe that's what they mean by *estranged.* "Daniel and Maggie are *estranged.*" I can't go on like this. I have to do something about it.

Liza

Athena's mother is driving me up the wall. Protective is one thing. Teri Shields is protective. Irini Georgopoulos is obsessed with Brooke Shields. She keeps telling me what Brooke earns, as if I didn't know what Brooke earns. So why haven't I made a movie deal for Athena? Athena isn't ready for a movie deal. Athena has only been modeling for a year, Brooke began at three months.

What's wrong with this woman? Athena is only sixteen years old. If I hadn't found her and groomed her, she'd still be in school, baby-sitting or working at McDonald's on weekends.

Irini has a bug up her ass about the upcoming California shoot. She wants to go along. I've told her the budget does not include extra people. That really set her off.

"I am not extra people."

It was not very diplomatic of me, I know, but I'm getting tired of her interference. More than that, it's her tone of voice—a high, penetrating whine like a vacuum cleaner.

I tried to mollify her. "Of course you're not extra people. You're the mother of America's hottest young model. Of course you worry about her and want to be with her." And want to protect your meal ticket. "But you must let your baby bird fly. I'll be there. I'll be sharing a suite with her. I'll be with her every minute. I'll never let her out of my sight."

Surely, Irini insists, Liza Central is making enough money out of Athena's young flesh to pay for one measly air fare and hotel room—meaning the money again, my agency commission. She has conveniently forgotten how they were living when I found them in a one-room apartment with a Pullman kitchen, Irini working as a saleswoman at A&S and barely making the rent.

I can see that in her heart of hearts, she really doesn't see why I should take a commission. I should work for them for the honor of it. She acts as if it's all coming to her. They're living on East Fifty-fourth Street in a sublet I found for them. No more subways to Brooklyn. She's running up bills at all the department stores and the Madison Avenue boutiques. Her phone bills are humongous. She speaks personally and for hours to everyone she's ever known in Greece, bragging about her success in America.

Her success. Athena has become her creation.

I ignore her suggestion that I absorb the cost of a trip to San Francisco. If she were another type of person, it wouldn't be that big a deal. Frankly, I don't want her along. She's disruptive. She interferes. Like the time she showed up at a party-dress shoot at the Cloisters for *Seventeen*. They had a *pro musica antiqua* group playing and singing love songs. The mood and setting were lyrical; everyone was caught up in the spirit of the damsel awaiting her lover, and Athena was so beautiful you held your breath.

The photographer's assistant was taking test shots with a Polaroid, and the lights and reflectors were being adjusted with infinitesimal care. But everyone froze in place—the stylist, the editorial crew from *Seventeen,* Myrna, and me—when Irini's voice rang out: "She looks sick."

"Please, Irini, we must be quiet. They're ready to shoot." I squeezed her arm as hard as I could to indicate the seriousness of the situation.

"Don't shush me. She looks like a corpse. She needs rouge. Let me."

Before I could stop her, she bolted in front of the camera,

blusher compact in hand. I grabbed her and yanked her back to the sidelines. "The makeup man has spent two hours on Athena's face."

"She looks dead. What are you trying to do?"

The photographer called out, "Liza, if this woman doesn't leave, I will."

I literally had to drag her outside. "Believe me, Irini. She will not look dead in the photographs. These are all top professionals. They know what they're doing."

Irini planted herself on a bench. "I'm waiting right here."

Exterior shots were coming up next. Myrna came out to say the *Seventeen* editor wanted a word with me.

"Irini, you have a choice. Either you will go back to my office and wait for us there, or you will go home and wait there. I don't care which—but you are not waiting here!"

As her mouth opened to protest, I put my verbal fist in it. "Athena's career is just starting. She can go a long way. But if the word gets out that she's difficult and that she has a pain-in-the-ass mother, believe me, that's it, the end of her career. Believe me, nobody has time for this."

She closed her mouth and let Myrna accompany her downtown in one of the hired cars. Fear of killing her golden gosling had kept her quiet for a while. Now, however, with the Revlon deal and the coverage in the *New York Times* and *Women's Wear Daily,* she has resurfaced like a cold sore.

"Liza should be ashamed," she told Myrna, a captive audience. "Stealing our money. What right has she got to such a big cut? Athena does all the work, Liza gets rich." Irini didn't have the nerve to say these things to my face, but she was working up to it, using poor Myrna as a sounding board. I could smell it coming, and I was doing my best to avoid a direct confrontation.

This morning, she caught me. Myrna was on long distance. I

picked up the next call. Big mistake; you never can tell who it will be. "Liza, it is urgent that I see you." Irini suggested dinner tomorrow night.

Tomorrow is Friday. Now I realize why I'm so depressed. Monday's a holiday, the schools are closed. Dan was saying he'd have to spend time with the girls. He's got me saying it, "the girls," as if they're anything in my life. They're not. Correction, they are. Two children. His children. What am I supposed to do, tell him not to see them, tell him it's a long weekend for me, too, and what am I supposed to do, knit a sweater?

I swore I'd never allow myself to think this way. It's no good, dammit. He's married. He's got to be with his kids. I can't wait till I go to California so I can think things over. On second thought, I don't need to think things over. I'm a smart girl, I know I can't go on like this. It can only get worse and I'm the one who will suffer. I'm going to tell him tonight. It's over. *Terminé. Finito.* Case closed. A married man is like junk food, a quick fix but bad for your health.

I've got to get my priorities straight. Two years from now, Athena Georgopoulos is going to mean more to my happiness than some married man on the make. Tonight, I am going to fuck the daylights out of him, and then I'm going to send him on his way, back to his wife and kids, a broken but wiser man.

Irini has a point. I have been avoiding her. I have jeopardized my relationship with my number one asset. Tomorrow night, I shall have dinner with Irini. I shall listen attentively to Irini. I shall charm the souvlaki off Irini and, if possible, become her best friend.

Success is its own aphrodisiac. I met Dan; I'll meet someone else.

Daniel

Maggie caught me totally by surprise. You could have knocked me over with a feather. I didn't know what to say. I was in the middle of reading the *Times* and drinking my coffee. All I could do was nod and say if that's what she wanted, it was okay by me.

The minute I left the house, I tried calling Liza from a phone booth. Myrna said she was having a power breakfast at the Regency. Even under normal circumstances, I don't feel comfortable calling her from my office. Sonia has a sneaky habit of strolling in when I'm in the middle of a conversation and making an elaborate pretense of not eavesdropping. That woman can hear a pin drop in the snow.

Besides, I wanted to be alone with Liza when I told her. When I rang her bell, she seemed to be waiting for me. The door flew open. The apartment was dark. She seemed to be wearing a cloud of some fluffy stuff that fell open in front, revealing her breasts. The door slammed behind me. She threw herself against me, her arms tight around my neck, her back warm and smooth and bare to the touch through the thin fabric.

"Daniel—I've been waiting!"

Beyond her entrance hall, candle glow from the living room formed a shimmery aura around her head and shoulders.

"Liza—what's going on?"

"If you don't know, I'm not doing it right." She was unbuttoning my jacket.

"Don't you see? The power of positive thinking. I didn't touch you, Dan. I literally didn't lay a finger on you, and you went off like a Roman candle. Now just think what would happen if I did touch you. Like this." She spit into her hands and applied the moisture to me with her palms in long, rhythmic strokes, as if working in wet clay at the potter's wheel.

Enough was enough. "Liza—" I struggled to free my arms.

"Don't move!" With her weight on my legs, I could not.

"Darling—"

"Don't darling me. You're my prisoner, remember? My love slave. How do you like that? I may just use you up like a tube of toothpaste. A little squeeze here, a little squirt there." She demonstrated. "And then, when you're all used up, all empty and useless, I'll just throw you away—into the garbage—like a squeezed-out toothpaste tube. If you were a soda can, I could at least get a rebate."

Suddenly, she was crying, and I was crying, too. The sadness in her voice, the anger, the sense of loss, reminded me of a woman I had once seen on the highway after an accident. A man, maybe her husband, lay on the verge covered in blood and shattered glass. In the distance I could hear an ambulance. The woman was dazed, but she couldn't stop pacing back and forth, bending over the man, yelling at him, kicking him, calling him an asshole.

"Liza, dear. Please—I've got something to tell you—"

"Later."

"Something important."

"Shut the fuck up!"

This wasn't Liza's style. She didn't talk like that. What the hell was going on? My jacket open, she yanked the shoulders back and down over my arms like a mugger, pinning my arms to my sides. I was helpless. I couldn't move. A tidal wave of excitement roared over me. I couldn't breathe. An undertow tore the ground out from under me. My knees buckled. My thighs tightened and fell away from my groin. I was hot and hard and gasping for air and totally off balance, and I would have slid to the floor if she hadn't held me upright and force-marched me backwards into the candlelit living room. I was disoriented. Pillows. There were a million pillows. I was on my back on a mountain of pillows, my arms still held prisoner by my jacket.

Her voice throbbed with quiet menace. This woman could kill me. Nobody knew where I was. She could kill me and nobody would ever connect us. The eerie thought excited me anew, but I didn't like it. I wanted her to stop the bullshit. "Liza—"

"Shut up, I said. Are you deaf or something? You've been ambushed, Daniel, taken prisoner. A prisoner of war. You had the balls to invade my sovereign territory, remember. You thought you won, didn't you? Thought you had a superior weapon, right? The supremacy of the cock, right? Well, let me show you a thing or two about sexual warfare."

The sound of a zipper in a muffled room is like a machine gun.

"Do you know what I'm going to do to you, Daniel?"

Despite myself, her words, her voice, were enough to send me through the roof. She sat astride my legs, her hands fanned out above me, fingers spread wide and swooping toward my groin like hungry birds that stopped just short of touching, her fingertips almost, but not quite, brushing me as I strained to meet them.

Now the tidal wave had invaded me, it was inside me, bottled up in the narrow culvert behind my gut, surging into the narrow passage, pounding through the swollen walls until bursting out into the open with a convulsion of such violence I thought I had turned inside out and was about to die.

When I opened my eyes, her face was close to mine. She was watching me intently with doctor eyes, as if to judge how I was responding to treatment.

I could not speak. I've secretly sneered at Frenchmen who speak of *le petit mort.* Now I know what they mean, "the small death." In that one cataclysmic moment, I had died and come back to life.

"You see?"

What? What did I see? What was she talking about? I wanted to take her in my arms, but my arms were still trapped. The game had gone on long enough.

"Liza, darling—"

"It's all your fault! You deserve to die!" Her face was contorted with fury, but her voice was like Liza's. Liza wanted me dead.

I managed to get up on one elbow and wriggle free of my jacket. Liza did not try to stop me. She rocked quietly back and forth like someone in mourning, but when I tried to embrace her, she sprang at me like a cheetah, clawing at the buttons of my shirt and calming somewhat when she got it off. Calmer still, she slid backwards in order to strip off my trousers and shorts.

"The socks. Should I leave on the socks? Naked men look obscene with socks. But we can't have you forget your socks again, can we? We don't want problems when you go home to your wife without your socks, do we?"

I kicked off the socks. "Screw the socks. Let me hold you, Liza. Please, sweetheart, let's stop this. I've got something important to tell you."

She knocked me back against the pillows. "Shut the fuck up,

I said, or didn't you hear me the first time? This is my party and I'll cry if I want to. I'm not finished with you. I'm going to make you beg for mercy, I'm going to make you wish you'd never met me. I am going to make you come until you die, you bastard, you scumbag, asshole, *creep!* You've got something to tell me? Well, I've got something to tell *you.* Get out of my life. Go home to your wife. It rhymes, godammit. There should be a law against married men. All men caught out with other women should be shot. Or castrated."

Her head dropped down on me as if to accomplish this with her teeth. Her shoulders shivered with sobs. She took me into her mouth in sad farewell, a bereavement, a goodbye to love.

I pulled her up and into my arms, a limp rag doll, all fight gone. "What is all this? I don't understand. I love you, Liza. I want to spend the rest of my life making you happy. I want only good things for us—the two of us—you and me—together. I pledge that by all that's holy. Please, darling, believe me. I'm so thankful I met you. I thank God every day for bringing us together. I swear to you, Liza. I didn't know what love is between a man and a woman until I found you. Please—say you believe me."

"I believe you."

"So what's all this about? Why are you acting this way? What did you want to tell me? Speak now or forever hold my piece."

"Bad joke."

"Agreed. Bad taste, too. Okay, my apologies. Your turn. What's on your mind?"

"You first, Dan. You had something to tell me."

This morning seemed long ago and far away in a distant land. Maggie had quite simply, without dramatics or explanation, informed me she was taking the girls to her brother's house in Phoenix for the long three-day weekend. She had not suggested I go with them. She didn't think I'd mind; the change might do us all some good.

"They're leaving tomorrow morning, Liza. It means we have Friday night, all day Saturday, Saturday night, all day Sunday, Sunday night, and all day Monday until I have to go to the airport to pick them up. Three whole days. Together. Just the two of us."

"Three whole days? Well, whoopee." The words were smart-ass, but she was clinging to me with her entire body, the way Sandi does when she's half-asleep and I cover her. I could not hurt Liza, ever, no more than I could hurt my little Sandi, or Jennifer, or Maggie either, for that matter. I would have to find a way.

"So, okay, Liza. Your turn."

Her gauzy garment spread out over us like spun sugar. She gathered it up and raised it above her waist to expose her nakedness as no other woman has ever revealed it to me. Other women have loved me or allowed me to love them. Maggie has done both and carried two babies to term by way of this same mysterious cave. Until Liza it was a place I had inhabited but never really seen. Neither shamefaced nor coy, Liza opened wide the portals and let me see the colors and contours of her private and personal self before taking me inside.

I'm yours, I wanted to tell her. I surrender completely, I wanted to say. But I didn't know how. I didn't have the vocabulary. I was afraid to say it, afraid to express the rapture of giving myself over to another human being.

I could hear strangled sounds in her throat like whimpering.

"Please, Liza, don't worry, it'll work out, I'm your man, I love you, we'll find a way, I promise. Don't cry."

"I'm not crying, you asshole."

She was riding me like a rodeo queen on a bucking bronco, high in the saddle, her knees gripping me hard, yips of triumph mixed with peals of laughter.

"Don't you see?"

"Don't I see what?"

"Don't you see what I was going to tell you? This was kiss-off night. I was telling you to get lost, to stop complicating my life. I was doing a Titanic on you, a night to remember. This was going to be it. I was never going to see you again."

Maggie

I hope I'm doing the right thing. Dan looked surprised, but he didn't try to talk us out of going—or suggest he go with us. Jennifer's always talking about needing space. Maybe Dan needs some space. I hope I'm not making a mistake leaving him alone like this; give a man enough rope and he'll hang himself. I don't want him to hang himself. I don't want him to tie a new knot, either. Maybe I'm making something out of nothing. Maybe I overreacted to Sonia.

She was sorry to be the one to tell me, but she thought I should know. Dan was playing around. It's funny how I instantly jumped to his defense. Ridiculous. Not ridiculous, she insisted. How did she know, had he told her? There was no need for sarcasm, Sonia said, she was only trying to help. Connie, her manicurist, had seen Dan and this other woman together, several times. Connie recognized Dan because she often came up to the office to do Sonia's nails. She was also a jogger. She had seen them running together morning after morning. She had seen them holding hands and kissing goodbye—and she had seen the two of them leaving Central Park together, heading toward the East Side.

Ridiculous, I repeated. Vicious gossip. How dare she take the word of a third-rate little manicurist. I had half a mind to call this Connie and tell her off. What I should really do, Sonia said, was call Connie and have her do something about my hair. Evidently, Connie was a superb hair colorist as well. Sonia said it was time to stop kidding myself that gray hair is glamorous with a young face. "That's baloney, Maggie dear. Gray hair makes every face old. And anyway, you're not that young."

Dan likes me the way I am, I defended myself feebly.

The girl in the park has thick reddish hair that bounces when she runs, according to Connie; the kind of hair a man wants to run through barefoot, Sonia added in her own inimitable way.

"Why are you telling me this, Sonia? I know you don't like me very much, but that's no reason to try and wreck my marriage."

"God, are you stupid! Where have you been—Mars? I'm trying to save your marriage. Not for your sake, I might add. For my own selfish reasons. I'll be honest with you. I want Dan to concentrate on business. I don't want him distracted with lawyers and settlements and all that. My advice to you is to do something—and quick, before it's too late."

I thanked her for her concern. I didn't think I should confront Dan with this information. Surely Sonia would not want me to tell him her manicurist had seen him with another woman in Central Park, now would she?

"It's your marriage, kiddo," Sonia said. She was just trying to be a friend, a word to the wife and all that. It was up to me to decide what to do.

That was nice of her, letting me decide. Frank and Helen had reminded me of their open invitation to visit. They had plenty of room, a swimming pool, two horses, and a pony Sandi could ride. Arizona was beautiful, sun and sky and wide-open spaces. They were at the airport to meet us, of course—tan, relaxed, exclaiming over how much the girls had grown and how pretty they both were. I caught a passing glance of worry in Helen's eyes before they crinkled into laughter. What I needed, she said, was to get out of those New York City clothes and have a margarita.

Dan had been included in their invitation. They accepted the excuse of too much work without comment and have not mentioned him again. They're my relatives. I'll have to watch myself. I've been close to tears ever since my conversation with Sonia. I don't want to break down in front of everyone. Helen senses something's wrong. She suggested the two of us run over to Scottsdale for the afternoon. Frank can take the girls riding, she said, while we women have a nice visit.

I have to talk to someone I can trust. I know Helen cares about me. Maybe she can tell me what to do. I'm so scared. I don't know what I'll do if I lose Dan. Just thinking about it makes me sick. But I've got to think about it.

Liza

It's crazy, I know. I should have stuck to my plan. I should get him out of my life, get rid of him, give him the old heave-ho. Nothing good can come of this, I'll be the loser, the man is married; but I can't help myself. I want him. I'm happy with him. No, happy's not the word. *Ecstatic* is more like it. This weekend is a gift from the gods. I should have said no but I want it, I want every minute we can be together. Three whole days together, alone, sleeping together in my bed, waking up together. I should have stuck to my plan, but what good would it do to cheat ourselves of this weekend? His family's away, so he'd be alone. I don't have any plans, so I'd be alone. We're not hurting anyone by being together; we're not taking anything away from Maggie and the girls. They're in Phoenix. We're here. Together.

I'm so energized I can't sit still. Dan just phoned from the airport. The plane just took off. He'll pick me up at eight. Shall we stay in? I ask. I've been scribbling a list of things to buy on the way home—daisies, Carr's biscuits, smoked salmon, capers, the good brown bread, brie, the almonds he likes, and a bottle of Batard Montrachet from Joseph Drouhin, and damn the cost.

No, he wants to take me out. He wants to put on a dark suit and a silk tie and he wants me to wear my prettiest dress and best perfume. What do I say to the Rainbow Room, high above Manhattan, the perfect place for lovers? Brilliant.

I am straightening my desk and thinking about bubble baths and garter belts when Myrna buzzes me to say Irini Georgopoulos is on the phone. I can't believe it. I have forgotten our dinner date. It went completely out of my head. What am I going to do? She'll kill me for canceling out. But I can't help it. Dan is taking me to the Rainbow Room. How can I spend three hours with this rat-faced, troublemaking cow when I could be dancing in Dan's arms? Why does this have to happen? All I want is a little happiness; is that too much to ask? If I'm being honest, I have only myself to blame. I got off on the wrong foot with Irini. I've been catering to her whims, placating her feelings. She should be catering to me. I'm the one who made Athena a star. Irini should be lighting candles for me.

Why am I making such a big deal about postponing a dinner date? Because in my gut I know business is business and I shouldn't be doing it. Irini will have a purple fit, but I can't help it. She'll simply have to wait till next week. Monday maybe, after Dan leaves for the airport to pick up the family.

Before I can begin to make excuses, Irini tells me there's a change in plan. *God is good.* What a shame, I say, I was so looking forward to seeing her, what about Monday night?

But the change in plan is that instead of dinner, we're going to a celebrity party on board Donald Trump's yacht—me, Athena, and herself. Everyone will be there. While I feverishly try to figure out how I can gracefully get out of it, it occurs to me to ask how she got invited. Celebrity invitations usually come to the agency.

She's hired a publicist, she informs me. She doesn't think Athena is getting sufficient exposure in the media—how quickly she's learned the jargon!—and one of things she wants to discuss is my absorbing the publicity fee, since after all, the agency will benefit.

The nerve of her, hiring a publicist without consulting me and then expecting me to pay for it. I stay cool. With as much charm as I can muster, I tell her how relieved I am that she and Athena have this great party to go to, that I've been worried sick and was just about to call her because a conflict has arisen, a business emergency, and I was trying to figure out how to put out the fire and also have dinner with her. Isn't it wonderful the way things work out? We wouldn't have had a chance to talk on the yacht. Why not have our quiet dinner on Monday?

The problem is she wants me to accompany them to the party. She has increasingly styled herself as the queen mother, and clearly she wants me and this new publicist and God knows who else as her entourage, paying court. I still feel threatened by older people giving me orders. However much I rebel, I'm still conditioned by mother's admonition that my mission in life is to please. I am still ready to submit for the sake of peace when other people try to push me around. After four years as the boss of my own enterprise, I have to keep reminding myself that Eileen Ford doesn't jump through hoops, so why should I.

I express the sincere hope that she and Athena enjoy their evening on the yacht and say that I look forward to seeing her Monday night. Myrna is afraid of Irini. She looks worried when I leave the office.

The Friday rush hour is in full gridlock. Only bicycles and pedestrians can function. I snake through the demented traffic, feeling giddily superior to the paralyzed BMWs and stretch limoes that can't move an inch. I weave effortlessly through the crowds in perfect urban stride, never missing a beat or having to stop. My mind fast-forwards to the weekend ahead—the flowers, the wine, the Rainbow Room, cold sheets, hot chocolate, three days and three nights of Dan and me with the entire lunatic city as our playground.

I tingle all over as I replay last night in slow motion. Dan says he has never experienced anything like it; he's never known a woman like me or made love the way we did. The same goes for me. I've never known I could be the woman I was and make love the way we did. So far, I've been smart enough not to tell him that.

I think of Irini and Athena on the Trump yacht. I'm probably missing out on making some valuable contacts, but *c'est la vie.* I deserve some personal happiness. For this weekend, I'm off the map.

Daniel

The woman is too much. On Saturday we walked downtown to the new antique center on Fifty-seventh Street and had what Liza calls a C & C—cappuccino and croissant—at the Delice downstairs. Passing Bergdorf's, she said, "I have an idea. Let's pretend you're my lover—"

"I am your lover."

"I mean my *kept* lover, my toy-boy—I'm the lady tycoon and your job is to sat-is-fy me—sex-u-al-ly—that's all—"

The woman is a witch, or else how could she know my secret fantasy? I've never told a soul how I've wondered what it would be like to be Claus von Bulow or Porfirio Ruberosa, a stud providing sex on demand, like in that movie *American Gigolo.*

"That's *all*—?" I grabbed her ass right there on Fifth Avenue and Fifty-seventh Street, not caring who might see us, caught up in Liza's game, clasping her to me and whispering in her hair. "What if I fucked you right here? What's in it for me? A Trans-Am? An Armani trenchcoat? What sorts of things do toy-boys get?"

She carried the game right into Bergdorf's. "I'm buying you a prezzie. Underwear. Men buy lingerie for their girlfriends, that's what I'm buying for you."

The red satin boxer shorts enthralled her. She and the saleswoman discussed the fabric and the workmanship intently, as if I were either invisible or too stupid to speak. Together they looked me over to ascertain the correct size.

"He'll try them on," Liza decided.

No way. Time to go.

Before I knew it, I was in the dressing room, trying on a pair of red satin boxer shorts. If I have to say so myself, I've got a great pair of legs. Liza was examining me as if I were a slipcovered sofa, fore and aft, patting and pulling with evaluating intensity.

"Daniel dear, it's *you!*" She crossed her eyes. "How do they *feel?*"

As a matter of fact, I've never had on satin underwear. It was turning me on. I could suddenly see why some men wore women's underwear.

Liza locked the dressing room door with a loud click. "Want to fool around?"

Too far, she was going too far. I'm just an ordinary guy. What was she trying to do to me? I felt like a horse's ass. "They have hidden cameras in these dressing rooms to stop you from shoplifting."

"So much the better. Let's give them something to see!"

"You're making fun of me, dammit."

Her entire mien changed. She cupped my face in her hands and smiled sadly. "I'm making fun of myself. I'm supposed to be this hot, sophisticated sexpot who's driving you wild with lust. I was just teasing. Forgive me, darling, I was afraid you might lose interest."

Cameras or not, I took her in my arms and assured her I would never lose interest, that I would love her for the rest of my life. She insisted on buying me the shorts. More subdued after that, we strolled up to the outdoor book mart on Central Park across from the Pierre and came face to face with another browsing couple. Liza's hand tightened in mine.

"Liza! What a surprise." He was tall, dark, lean, and ten years younger than me, with the veneer of success all over him; the woman with him was petite, blonde, and cracking bubble gum. They were wearing matching outfits, white cableknit sweaters and jodhpurs. I had the grotesque feeling they knew I was wearing red satin shorts.

"Hi, Mark."

"I think you know Tiffany."

Liza pressed against me in a proprietary way. "This is Daniel."

He nodded at me suspiciously.

"We're in a hurry," Liza said.

"Well, so are we!" He pushed angrily past us, the blonde in tow. She was a cool one. She turned long enough to blow an enormous bubble and pop it at Liza.

"Oh, look what I've found!" Liza made a big show of picking up a book from a secondhand table. "Dorothy Parker's poems. I think it's a first edition. Look at this. Viking, 1936. Can you imagine?"

I took the book and replaced it on the table.

"What was that all about?"

"What was what all about?"

"That man—that couple."

"That man was my ex-husband, and that was the younger woman he was—is—screwing!"

There was nothing I could say. I think it occurred to us both that she was the younger woman I was screwing. She bought the Dorothy Parker as a gift for her mother. We walked all the way back to her place, stopping to buy food and pick up a movie. We cooked dinner, played tapes, and she actually made a point of telling me to call Phoenix and see how everyone was, closeting herself in the bedroom so as not to inhibit me.

Helen answered the phone and said how sorry she was I couldn't make it. I did not tell her Maggie had not invited me. The girls got on the extension and told me excitedly about the horses, Sandi wanting to know why we can't have a horse.

Maggie, it seemed, was baking a pie, her hands full of flour. She couldn't come to the phone. She'd see me Monday.

That night, Liza and I slept in each other's arms, but we didn't make love. On Sunday we did the puzzle and went to the museum, saying very little, and what we did say seemed forced. What I really wanted to do was go home. Not that I didn't love Liza or want to be with her, but I realized I was exhausted, emotionally and sexually pooped. I didn't know what to do or what to say.

She had that preoccupied look on her face. I could see the wheels turning. "What's wrong, Liza? Anything bothering you?" I thought it might be her ex-husband but was afraid to ask.

"I'm sorry." She put her arms around me. "It's Athena—her mother, really. Let's not talk about it, shall we? This is our special weekend. I'm not bringing the office home."

Monday being a holiday, we had planned to maybe sleep late, watch the parade, and hang out until it was time for me to hit the road for the airport. The aroma of coffee woke me early. Liza was dressed and reading the *Times.*

"Fucking son of a bitch!"

She had the paper folded to the social page.

"What's going on?"

A photograph taken aboard the Trump yacht showed Athena and her mother huddled in rapt conversation with international model mogul Johnny Casablancas and his supermodel Paulina, whose contract with Estée Lauder alone was worth five million dollars. Casablancas had his arm around Irini and was listening earnestly to her.

"Look at him. He's romancing Irini. He's going after Athena. Dammit, I should have been there!"

Our eyes met. She looked stricken. "I didn't mean that. I wanted to be with you more than anything. This weekend means everything to me, but I can't let that snake steal Athena. I don't know what I mean. It's not fair. Can't I have love *and* a career? It's Irini, the ungrateful bitch. I spend two years on Athena and she's playing kneesies with Johnny Casablancas!"

"But don't you have a contract?"

She looked at me as if I were retarded. "It's like a marriage contract. If someone wants to leave, you can't stop them."

"Maybe let's skip lunch," I said.

We smiled sheepishly at each other. Holiday or not, it was Monday. Both our offices were officially closed, but each of us was itching to be there. I, for one, had some overdue calls to make to Europe, and I had left my office in chaos in my hurry to leave on Friday. It seemed so long ago. Maggie and the girls would be getting ready to leave Phoenix. I had a few clear hours of work before leaving for the airport.

On the walk downtown, the intimacy we had lost seemed to return. A rush of feeling overtook me. I was in love with this woman. "Let's go back. Let's have another few hours together."

She pulled me into a Madison Avenue doorway. "I'm so glad you said that!" Tears filled her eyes. "I thought we'd lost it. Oh, darling, I'm so confused. This weekend—it was too heavy, we tried to make every second count. It was too much—you can't sustain the high. Something's got to give. I can't stand much more of this."

Was she kissing me off? I couldn't blame her if she was. I didn't know whether to be sorry or relieved. "Does this mean you don't want to see me anymore?"

At that moment, a taxi pulled up to let someone out. Liza made a dash for it and jumped inside. "Speak to you later!"

Liza

My mother always talks about men having "appetites," meaning they're being led astray by their "appetites." For example, the Duke of Windsor: she's never forgiven the Duke of Windsor for giving up the crown for the woman he loved. She's constitutionally unable to say the word *cock,* but that's what she means when she talks about Wallis Simpson leading him around by the nose.

"That's where women have it over the men, Liza. We're not led astray by our appetites. The woman who puts a man first is asking for trouble. Listen to your mother."

Listening is not a deterrent. It is merely a reminder. The lesson of the weekend was crystal clear, a message of conscience, if not from God above. In choosing a dirty weekend with a married man over my responsibility to my top model, I have jeopardized my entire future. I should have been at Irini's side. I should have been the one with the protective arm around her when Johnny Casablancas came by. God knows what was said, though I have a pretty good idea.

Tonight's dinner with Irini was going to be rough. I would have to eat humble pie without demeaning myself. The woman was shrewder than I thought. The first thing to do was telephone and congratulate her on having her picture in the paper. And tell her how beautiful she looked. And that she photographed well enough to be a model herself. Johnny Casablancas probably told her that already.

Athena answered the phone. Her mother was resting. She had left a message if Liza called. She could not have dinner tonight. Athena sounded nervous. I could hear a man and woman laughing and talking in the background.

"What's going on, Athena?"

"Leave me out of this."

"Athena, I can guess what's going on. I know your first loyalty is to your mother. I'm your friend as well as your agent. If you want to call me or see me, I'm here."

There was no response.

"Athena? Are you there?" A horrible thought flashed through my mind. She had at least a hundred thousand dollars in bookings before we left for California. "You have your schedule for tomorrow, right? I have it right in front of me and I can read it to you again if you like." Still no reply. "Athena?"

"Yes." Barely audible.

"You will show up, won't you?"

Silence.

"Athena, if there are problems, we can work them out. If you switch agents that's something else. But if you fail to meet a commitment, you'll ruin your reputation in the industry. There's too much money involved. It doesn't matter how good you are, nobody will hire an unreliable model."

She was still on the line. I could hear breathing.

"Tell you what, you're due at Scavullo's at nine. Why don't I swing by for you in a cab so we can talk about California?" As if an afterthought, I added, "And tell Irini I've figured out a way for her to come along. As a consultant."

Never again. Never, ever, would I lose sight of my priorities. I hadn't heard the danger signals because I wasn't listening. If I had lost Athena, it was my own damn fault. *Sex!* Nature's mockery. Kisses don't buy condominiums. Orgasms don't buy happiness. The Beatles proved money can't buy love; but on a rainy day it's nice to order a limo.

I've got to put all my energies into work. I've got to hang onto Athena. I've got to develop new talent. My mother always said I was lazy. She's right. I've been lazy. I've got to hit the trail again, go to student fashion shows, find embryo talent, the fourteen- and fifteen-year-olds, get 'em while they're young.

Dan is past tense. Not on the back burner. Not on hold. Off the map. Tonight I go to bed early. Tomorrow I'm up at the crack to call for Athena and stay with her all day. I'll have Myrna send Irini flowers—stinkweeds, the bitch.

What I really should do is have liposuction on my brain to get rid of the fat. How stupid can you be, making a major romance out of an affair, a sneaky little affair with a married man. Seeing Mark with the Bubble Gum Kid put everything in focus. I'm divorced, but seeing them together, I'm a wife. A part of me will never recover from finding them together in bed. Dan's got a wife, so I'm the Bubble Gum Kid—and I don't like myself.

It was over. I would not see him again. I was about to go home when I realized my office *was* my home, where I really lived. My apartment was where I slept—and screwed around with married men. But no more! As I set the burglar alarms before leaving, a messenger arrived with a letter from Irini's new publicist, Billy Gray Tatham. It informed me that pursuant to his client's instructions, he would henceforth be the clearinghouse for Athena's media interviews, charity appearances, and the like. He closed by saying he felt sure he could count on my cooperation; his signature was scribbled initials in lieu of his name. In the lower left-hand corner was a "cc": Irini Georgopoulos.

Daniel

Halfway home from the airport with Sandi on my lap, Jennifer looking twenty-five in a Stetson and fringed jacket, and Maggie also looking twenty-five and freckled, I realized I was wearing the red satin shorts. What if we had an accident? I stared prayerfully at the driver's head. *Please slow down, please stop tailgating.* I could see it all—the ambulance, the emergency room, the nurses stripping me and bursting into hysterics.

"You look tired," my wife said.

Safely arrived at the apartment, I realized I must look stupid, too. I had not been home since Friday. Mail and newspapers were stacked at the door. Maggie made no comment. Was she blind? Even a blind man could see nobody had been there. I've seen enough movies about cheating husbands covering their tracks. I should have come home before going to the airport, dropped wet towels on the bathroom floor, used up the toilet paper and not replaced it, scattered newspapers on my side of the bed, left dirty dishes in the sink. Then she'd have really known I was up to something. That's not the way I live.

The girls were too busy with themselves to notice. Maggie went to the kitchen to make coffee. I made for our bathroom. I had to do something about the shorts. It wasn't as if I do a striptease undressing in front of Maggie, but we're married long enough to walk around in our underwear.

Just as I dropped my pants and took off the shorts, Maggie tapped on the door. Could I hand out the aspirin? I could hand her the aspirin, all right, but I could not go back into the bedroom to get a clean pair of shorts because I could hear her unpacking.

"You okay?" she called.

"Be right out." I flushed the toilet twice to confirm my activity.

I had no choice but to forget about shorts and zip up my pants. I was so nervous, I caught some hairs in the zipper and had to use Maggie's nail scissors to snip myself free without doing further damage.

I turned on the sink faucets and made splashing sounds while I tried to figure out how to get rid of the red satin shorts. They were too thick to flush down the toilet. If I'd had time, I could have cut them into pieces with the nail scissors. Then there was the laundry hamper—too dangerous. Back from a trip, Maggie might decide to do a wash tonight, and then what would I say?

A charitable breeze sensed my panic. It riffled the curtains on the bathroom window. I rolled the shorts into a ball and pitched it as hard and as wide as I could, praying nobody had seen me. The thought struck me that some homeless man might pick it up and enjoy the exotic pleasure of satin underwear.

It had been quite a weekend. Liza's right. We can't go on like this. I think we had to go through this to get it out of our systems. It's over and done. I don't want Maggie to know anything about it. Those shorts nearly gave me away, like I wanted to be caught, like I wanted to be punished, which is not the case at all. More than anything, this weekend has proved to me I'm a family man. I've missed my wife and daughters and our home. I'm happy to have them back. I've been a bastard, and I'm going to do everything I can to make it up to them.

Maggie

Helen said I was right to take off for a few days. All the signs pointed to an affair. The best thing was to let it run its course, to give him some space to do whatever he wanted to do without having to sneak around. Freedom is a frightening thing to married men. They may wish they were bachelors chasing the girls, but when they get the chance they remember how nice it is at home.

Most important, she warned, was to ignore obvious signs—makeup on his shirts, late-night walks to get the paper so he can use a pay phone, credit card charges. "Don't ask questions. Don't demand explanations. You're the three little monkeys. You see no evil, speak no evil, hear no evil." That was, of course, assuming I still wanted him.

I still want him. I've dumped out the sour milk and watered the kitchen plants. We've agreed to send out for pizza and eat in the kitchen. I'm setting the table when Daniel comes in. "I'm glad you're home, Maggie."

Me, too.

Liza

Things are back on track—for the time being, at least. Athena was waiting downstairs when I called for her. Always so quiet around Irini, she was obviously excited to be on her own and chattered away in the taxi.

I thought I was being tactful by mentioning Johnny Casablancas in general terms. "I'm sorry I wasn't there when you met him. Elite is one of the biggest model agencies in the world. He and Eileen Ford practically divide the territory, but there's still room for a few mini-agencies like mine. I hear he's dynamite to be with."

She looked at me the way she looks into the camera, her dark blue eyes conveying a wisdom and compassion beyond her years—The Look advertisers want to sell their messages.

"He makes my skin crawl. I feel comfortable with you. Don't mind my mother. It's hard having a beautiful daughter—nobody pays any attention to you."

From now on, Irini would be smothered with attention. She couldn't quite get herself to thank me for the flowers, but she did acknowledge their arrival. As for California and my sick fear she would cancel Athena out, she deigned to accept the invitation to join us, although not without making me eat shit: "Are you sure I won't be a nuisance, Liza? I really wouldn't want to get in the way. Be honest now, I wouldn't dream of going unless you really want me." She finally gave in and allowed me to convince her. The deciding factor was a matched set of airplane luggage with her initials in gold.

The shoot was three weeks away. I had asked Dan to make all the travel arrangements, and his staff had done a great job of block-booking at the lowest discount. Just because we were not seeing each other personally was no reason not to do business, at least this once. I would not have to talk to him. Myrna called him to add Irini's arrangements.

For the first time in days, I could take a deep breath. This morning, I went jogging for the first time since the weekend. Sure enough, he was there. He looked anxious when he saw me. What did he think I was going to do, knock him down and dry-hump him? I nodded "Hi" and kept on going.

When I got to the office, my mother was on hold.

"She said she was reading the paper and would wait," Myrna said.

"Mark called me."

Mine is the only divorce in America where my mother and ex-husband are bosom buddies. I should have given him custody of her.

"He said he saw you with some man. It looks serious, he said."

"What business is it of his? He was with the gum-chewer." I didn't rush to the phone to tattle on him to his mommy.

"Is it serious?"

"Maybe—"

"So why haven't you told me? Why haven't I met him?"

I hesitated just long enough for my mother to get the picture.

"He's married! Is that it? Of course that's it, that's why you're keeping it a secret."

"Well, it's my secret. I'm a big girl now. I'm responsible for my own life."

"Mark said he had a gut feeling the guy was married."

"Tell Mark to soak his head."

"He is worried about you, Liza. He still loves you. He's told me so. The divorce should never have happened. It was all a big mistake."

The divorce wasn't the mistake. Getting married was the mistake. Men are the mistake. I was finished with Dan, but I didn't want to give my mother the satisfaction of telling her that.

"You know what your trouble is, Liza?"

Here we go.

"Your trouble is you're too damned independent, too smart for your own good. You girls today don't understand marriage. The only way a woman can be happily married is if she's totally dependent on her husband."

"Mother!"

"Shut up. I'm talking. The whole thing is an act. Women know it's an act. Men don't know it's an act. Women my age understand that."

"So how come women your age are getting dumped? All your sixty-year-old girlfriends are getting shafted when hubby dyes his chest hair and takes up with his secretary!"

"They forgot it was an act. Life is an act. The woman who acts totally dependent is usually smarter than her husband. He's the breadwinner, sure, but she earns her way by pretending she can't change a light bulb without him."

"Mother, I don't believe what I'm hearing."

"Believe it. It's all an act. I'm acting right now. I am acting your mother. Do you think I enjoy playing a sixty-two-year-old mother? I'm not ready for the shawl and carpet slippers. But you're my daughter and I love you and my job is to be your mother."

"But what you're saying is so unfair, so dishonest. Men and women should love each other honestly."

"Listen to you. Are you crazy? Is that what they taught you in college? You should never have thrown Mark out. So what if he was *schtupping* some little tramp? You don't let a man like Mark slip through your fingers."

"I have another call, Mom. Speak to you later."

"It's a good thing you're making money. You'll be able to buy yourself a husband."

Daniel

I want to make love to her, but I can't. My own wife—beautiful, loving, sweet, patient. I know how to make her happy, but I can't get it together. She's so goddam understanding. She knows how hard I've been working, how much stress I've been under . . . She doesn't know anything. I'd like to tell her, I'd really like to tell her about Liza and wipe that saintly smile off her face. Poor Maggie, she's everything a good wife's supposed to be, everything a man could ever want.

I can't cut it. I can't get Liza out of my system. She's in my blood. I can't stop thinking about her and wanting her. This morning in bed in one of those dreams before waking, I relived every moment of that incredible candlelit night. I was moaning with pleasure when I woke up to find Maggie shaking me and asking if I was okay. I don't know if I called out Liza's name.

I'll simply have to tough it out. When I saw her at the reservoir yesterday, I tried to talk to her. She said "Hi" like I was a stranger and kept moving.

Then when Myrna called about the California trip, I thought Liza was canceling out. I couldn't have blamed her, even though I had had my whole shop working on it for days. If she wanted nothing more to do with me, that was that. But all Myrna said was to add Athena's mother to the booking.

"Is Liza around? I'd like to have a word with her."

"She's in a meeting."

Sonia has just wandered into my office. Her private radar must have picked up on the emotional undercurrents of my call.

"No problem. Give her my regards."

Liza

This last week has been a bitch. I should have listened to my mother and become a teacher—a nice, safe profession with benefits and pensions. *And switchblades and crack.* Nothing's perfect, only now I'm convinced the whole world's insane. The company that commissioned me to package the California shoot called to say they looked at my figures and they have someone who could have done it cheaper, the CEO's sister-in-law, who's in the travel business. Someone always has a relative somewhere who can do things better, and it's politic to be polite.

The trip is in ten days. They wondered if it was too late to cancel the arrangements and have her do it instead. Ordinarily, I might have gone into a big song and dance about the difficulties, the penalties, and the insurmountable problems they were creating—and what's more pointed out that Dan's discounts were the biggest in town. I could have groveled and whined.

Instead, I said, "No. It's too late." Perhaps she could handle things next time. If there was a next time. This was to be Athena's last big booking before her exclusive arrangement with Revlon. Or before Johnny Casablancas lured her away from me.

I congratulated myself on standing firm, on giving a straightforward no instead of going around the mulberry bush. It's a lesson in business tactics I'm still learning. Just because a client suggests something doesn't mean you've got to agree. Otherwise, why should they hire you?

That resolved, I thought of Dan's reaction if I canceled. His computer system would go up in smoke. I'm still not over him. It's going to take time. The best thing is to keep busy. My mother's the problem now. I've told her a million times I'm not seeing Dan anymore, and furthermore, I want her to quit discussing me with Mark.

In that spirit, I called Mark.

"Liza. What a nice surprise."

"I'll get right to the point. I will only say this once. Do not, emphasis *not,* discuss me with my mother. In other words, bug out!"

Maggie

I don't know what happened while we were away, but whatever it was, he's been an absolute lamb since we got back. Home early every night. Helping the kids with their homework. Last night, he pulled out the old Scrabble board. I can't remember the last time we played. He made a big show of being intimidated by my superior vocabulary and made a lot of obvious mistakes in order to let me win, like he's trying to make up to me for something.

He still goes running in Central Park every morning. If Sonia was right and he was meeting someone there, he's not doing it anymore. He's back home almost before he leaves. Maybe it's my new hair color that's making me irresistible. It's one of those temporary no-peroxide wash-away-gray tints. I was tempted by deep auburn, but timid soul that I am, I settled for light ash brown.

I hate to admit Sonia's right about anything, but she did hit the nail on the head about one thing. I had sold myself a bill of goods that gray hair looks great on a young face. The light ash brown takes ten years off me. Jennifer and Sandi have noticed. The three of us have been waiting for Dan to say something.

That afternoon in Scottsdale, alone with Helen, I told her what Sonia had said. "Was I right to leave him alone?"

"It's hard to say. Give a man enough rope—"

"And he'll hang himself!" we chorused together. She made me feel so much better—women helping women to help themselves.

Tonight, Daniel actually went out of his way to compliment me on my dinner, the *blanquette de veau* he loves. When he went a step further and offered to help clear the table, the girls clutched at themselves with shrill giggles.

"It's worked!" Jennifer's whisper could be heard in Brooklyn.

"It worked!" Baby sister joined in.

"What worked? What's going on here? What are you guys up to?"

"Mommy's hair!" Sandi shouted.

"Are you blind, Daddy?"

With his hands on my shoulders, my husband looked at me, really looked at me. "I must be blind. I knew there was something different, but I didn't know what. You look beautiful, Maggie. Doesn't she, girls? How lucky can a man be to have three gorgeous women all to himself!"

We stood there in the dining room, the four of us with our arms around one another. Suddenly I realized Daniel was kissing me for real, a soft, demanding kiss full on the mouth, his tongue gently forcing my lips to part. It was so unexpected, I felt like a kid on my first date.

One of Helen's suggestions for saving my marriage was a last-chance baby before my time clock stops entirely. I'm tempted, and I'll see where his kisses lead us later tonight in bed. On the other hand, my new hair may have given me the courage to do what I've been wanting to do for fifteen years—go back to work.

Daniel

I had to talk to her, if only for a minute, if only to say our goodbyes like civilized people. The way she jumped into that cab and sped off like that—that's no way to end a relationship. I agree with her it couldn't work and we had to stop seeing each other, but we should have talked it out and wished each other luck, like civilized people.

Civilized, sure. Here I was lurking in the bushes waiting for her to show up at the reservoir.

"Liz, I've got to talk to you."

"You scared me, you jerk. I thought you were a mugger. Leave me alone."

She took off at a run instead of a trot. Instead of pursuing her, I ran in the opposite direction. In a minute we were face to face.

"Get lost, Dan. Get out of my face. I do not wish to see you. *Capisce?*"

"Five minutes, that's all. One minute. After what we've been to each other—the things we've done to each other—you can spare me one precious minute of your precious time."

"You shut the fuck up. How dare you talk about the 'things we've done to each other'? You are a Class B turd. I do not keep records or charts. I am not selling the rights to the *National Enquirer*. What we did we did for love and now it's over. Out of my way."

Yes, she's beautiful when she's mad. Yes, I wanted to jump on her bones right there, that minute, and the hell with who's watching. They might learn something.

"One question, Liza. Answer me one question and I'll go quietly."

"Okay. One question."

"Did you love me even a little?"

Her eyes clouded. "I loved you a lot."

I feel like that toothpaste tube, squeezed flat.

Maggie

I guess I expected too much. After so many years of marriage and the tensions of the past weeks, it was hard to become lovers again, the passionate lovers his kisses seemed to promise. The situation disintegrated into apologies. Each of us tried to take the blame.

"My fault."

"I've got a lot on my mind."

Still, I won't look a gift horse in the mouth. He's been affectionate and kind and home every night. Helen said all the signs are good and I should suggest a marriage counselor.

Instead of blowing his stack at the idea, Daniel was hangdog. "I'm trying to be a good husband," he said.

He certainly has been trying, and that's enough for me. Another baby is not the answer. This morning I decided I would talk about getting a job when he got back from the park. I had marked a few possibilities in the *Times* and wanted his advice. He looked strange when he came in, with an unhealthy flush in his face, like he was coming down with a fever. He refused to let me take his temperature or to stay home from the office.

"It's the running. Too much for an old man like me." He said he was going to quit and buy an Exercycle instead.

"You need a vacation," I sympathized. "You've been working much too hard."

"It's the busy season."

"It's always the busy season. Sonia takes off on vacations, why shouldn't you?"

"You're absolutely right. I'll talk to Sonia today."

His evident fatigue aroused my maternal concern. "You're kidding. I mean it. You saw how much good it did for me and the girls. Maybe you should get away for a few days of total relaxation." My mind was racing ahead. "You know—a health spa with a golf course and tennis courts, massages, something like that."

His face brightened. "You mean go away somewhere by myself without you and the girls? You wouldn't mind?"

"Of course we'd mind, but I think it would do you good. Only for a week, mind you."

"Sonia would kill me if I stayed away longer than that."

"I would kill you, too."

"We-ell—"

There was an expression on his face I could not quite fathom. If this wasn't my husband and if I didn't know him inside out, I would say there was a hint of cunning around the eyes, like the Big Bad Wolf cartoon in Sandi's book.

"Well, what? Salmon fishing in Scotland? A dude ranch in Texas? I'm getting envious. Maybe I shouldn't let you out of my sight."

It was too late. What I had wanted him to suggest was hiring a sitter so the two of us could have a second honeymoon. As usual, it was my own damned fault, suggesting he take a vacation by himself. What made me say things like that? The fragile hope that a brief separation would make his heart fonder?

"As a matter of fact, there are some new developments I've been wanting to check out on the West Coast, a new cruise line out of San Francisco, some luxury tours of Steinbeck country I want to monitor before recommending to clients. What I might do is spend a few days looking things over, making sure that what those fancy brochures say is accurate, and then maybe I'll drive down the Pacific Coast Highway to L.A. and fly back from there. What do you think?"

What I think is I'd like to go, too. What I said was, "Sounds great to me." Another black mark for childhood etiquette training. I've spent my life politely waiting to be asked.

His fatigue had disappeared. I could almost see the energy coursing through his veins. "Maggie, you're wonderful. It's just what I need, a few days on my own in California."

Liza

At last—the plane's starting to take on passengers. I'm so wiped out, I wish I had the nerve to ask for a wheelchair. Maybe I'll be able to catch some *z's* once we're airborne. I was up and down all night, going over all the details in my mind, all the tickets checked and double-checked, vegetarian meals for Athena and the other models, limousines ordered for those not driving their own cars to the airport. Poor Myrna, I drove her bananas yesterday: "Do this, do that, did you check that, are you sure—" She came through fine. I think I'll give her a raise. She put up with me without a murmur.

It didn't help me sleep. I kept thinking I'd forgotten something, like the time I took Athena to Paris for the showing of the collections and we were at the airport when she said she didn't have her passport. Fortunately for us, the plane was delayed, and Myrna raced back to the apartment and got back to the airport just in time.

Alone in bed, I wondered, is it worth it? My entire body was stressed out, every inch of me hurt, including my hair. My eyelids were lined with sand. *Panty hose!* Had I packed enough panty hose? Panty hose are like good wine. They do not travel. I never get runs in my panty hose in New York. The minute I leave town, every pair I put on pops on contact. A similar thing happens with shoes: beyond New York City limits, heels snap.

My bed looked like a war zone—pillows, blankets, sheets awry, my restless churning so severe that even the fitted sheet and mattress cover were wrenched from their anchorage. I noticed my teddy bear watching me from the bookshelf. That's what I needed, I thought, a nice little cuddle; but as I reached for him, his little face seemed to say, "Now you want me. Now that you don't have Dan."

Crying released some of the tension; it didn't make me feel that much better. It was the middle of the night, I was leaving on a major trip, a lot was riding on it, and dammit I wanted someone I loved to hold me in his arms and tell me not to worry, everything would be great. Why was that too much to ask? I thought of Mark in bed with Tiffany, and Dan in bed with Maggie, and couples together in every single bed in the entire world except mine.

It was no use. At four o'clock I got out of bed for good, ate a pint of cherry vanilla ice cream, put on a tape of *Casablanca,* did my floor exercises, watered the African violet plant that had survived the divorce, made the bed, wrote a note for the superintendent to say I'd be away, redid my toes and fingernails, got dressed, stuck my fingernail through my panty hose, broke my favorite lipstick, and was downstairs in the lobby ten minutes before the limo was due.

The good news is that Irini changed her mind about coming—at the last minute of course, so I'll have to pay for her ticket. Having won her point, she doubtless had second thoughts. Being on a shoot is tedious at best, especially if you have nothing to do but watch.

Athena has the seat next to mine. The captain has switched on the No Smoking-Fasten Your Seatbelt sign. In the harsh glare of the morning sun, her face is breathtaking. Free of makeup, her features are so beyond perfection as to be unreal. Perhaps she is the goddess Athena sprung from the head of Zeus, the virgin deity worshipped for her wisdom. I wonder if she is still a virgin and how wise she might be. I wonder how her face would look to a man making love to her. I've often worried about how my own face looks in the throes of passion—whether I look grotesque and whether that's a good reason for turning the lights off.

For some reason, the thought cheers me. I haven't had any complaints. I showed Dan a few tricks, didn't I? He's still in shock. I found him; I'll find somebody else.

Sonia

All of a sudden Dan's going to San Francisco. Something's up. He can't fool me. When he can't look me in the eye, I know he's up to something. The Alaska cruise lines? Steinbeck country? What's he talking about? There's no reason in hell for him to go all the way out there to check them out! They're all reliable packagers, in business for years. Something's cookin', and it ain't kosher.

Then, it hits me like a ton of bricks—one of the new clients he's brought in, the model agency. A nice piece of change, group booking for sixteen people, air transportation, hotels, ground transfers, the works. A big fashion catalog, he said, on location all this week. Where? We're talking Marin County, we're talking north of San Francisco.

The client contact is Myrna. Is Myrna the girl Connie saw him with in the park? Could little Myrna be the reason he's been walking around with a long face like his best friend died? Wouldn't it be a coincidence if Myrna whatever-her-name-is also happened to be in San Francisco?

There was one way to find out. Using as an excuse that the travel arrangements were our first assignment and I wanted to be sure everything was okay, I asked for Myrna, fully expecting to be told she was in San Francisco. She was not. She was right here in New York City. She thanked me for calling and said she would pass along my message when Liza phoned in from San Francisco. She assumed I knew who Liza was.

I do now.

Liza

It's a wrap—four days of shooting, six locations, forty-eight changes, including makeup and accessories. The weather held, the hairspray held, the tempers held. There was only one tantrum—mine, when I left my makeup bag in a roadside ladies room and didn't realize it until an hour later. Athena lent me hers. This trip has made us friends. Without Irini around, she was a sweet, affectionate teenager, coming to me for assurance, working patiently without complaint with the stylists and dressers to make lightning-fast changes.

Tonight's wrap party was in Chinatown. Athena called for attention and proposed a toast. Along with the others, I raised my glass.

"To Liza!" she said. "The best friend and the best agent in the entire world. Eileen Ford . . . Elite . . . Wilhelmina . . . make way for Liza."

All I could do was stammer my thanks and return the compliment. "To Athena. Who gives new meaning to beauty, a beautiful person both inside and out, and next year's number one supermodel. Paulina . . . Anuschka . . . Christie . . . Isabella . . . and of course, Brooke! . . . watch out for Athena."

By tomorrow night, we'd all be back in New York, going our

separate ways. After dinner, Athena and I wandered through Haight-Ashbury, the Hashbury of the sixties Flower Children. Not much was left to bear witness to those days except the City Lights bookstore. I was too young to be there during the Beat Poets heyday, but one of the first gifts of love Mark ever gave me was Lawrence Ferlinghetti's *A Coney Island of the Mind,* which he read to me one night as we sat facing each other in his bathtub.

He swiped the book when we split up. He denied it vehemently and accused me of malice for accusing him. Whatever the truth, it was gone. Now I bought myself a new one and turned to our favorite, "I Am Waiting," page forty-nine. The poem was there, but not the stains of love and bath oil. I will never forgive Mark. Yet, the book in my hand, however pristine, reminded me as always that I am still waiting for a rebirth of wonder.

Later, in Ghiardelli Square, dutiful daughters that we are, we bought gifts for our respective mothers. Neither of us had a man to shop for, she because she had not yet left the nest, I because the man I had married had dumped on me and swiped my books, and the man I loved was married, and that was that.

While I was trying to choose a scarf my mother would not immediately give to the cleaning lady, Athena disappeared. A few minutes later, she pressed a tiny package into my hand. It was a stylized mother-of-pearl fish made into a pendant on a slender silver chain. "I want to thank you for all you've done for me, Liza."

I was quite overcome. I get pissed off when people don't appreciate me. When someone does, I dissolve. It took a supreme effort of will to keep from blubbering in front of my young protégée.

"You've got The Look, Athena. You're going to be a superstar. If I hadn't found you, somebody else would have, believe me, somebody like Johnny Casablancas."

Her face hardened.

"Don't pay any attention to my mother. Johnny Casablancas has been sending her stuff—champagne, chocolates from Godiva, a basket of Greek delicacies, olives, taramasalata, fresh feta, stuffed grape leaves—"

"Is that why she stayed in New York?"

A flush of guilt suffused her cheeks.

"I told her I want to stay with you. You found me that day at the souvlaki stand. You made me what I am today. I don't care what he says he can do for me. I'm sticking with you."

Back in my room at the Mark Hopkins, I felt overwhelmed by the same aloneness that had assailed me the night before we left New York. There were no messages waiting for me, no lover calling to say he missed me and couldn't wait for me to get back and what did I want to do over the weekend. I could enjoy the onanistic pleasure of sleeping alone in a luxurious hotel room thousands of miles from home; and I dreaded the thought of my New York bed. There's such a thing as too much room to stretch. Damn you, Mark, why couldn't you behave yourself? And screw you, too, Daniel, the park isn't safe with men like you looking to score. I don't want to sleep alone the rest of my life. I want a man of my own.

Maggie

Sonia thinks she's hoodwinking me when she's syrupy on the phone. It would be laughable if it weren't so insulting. "How *are* you and the girls making out with Dan away?" Her voice oozes insincerity like W. C. Fields's.

"Oh, we're near death from malnutrition. We need him to turn on the stove and open the refrigerator for us."

"You're *what?"* she bellows into the phone before pretending to laugh. "Oh—I see—you're joking. If there's one thing I've got it's a sense of humor."

It's a good thing I have one, too, as she applies the soft soap—how young I look, how gorgeous, and what a figure, just like a young girl's, who'd guess I have two grown-up children, there must be a portrait of me in the attic, "like Dorian Leigh." It's Dorian Gray, Sonia. I do not correct her. She's leading up to something and I don't want to distract her.

She's like certain women you see in a shoe salon. They try on every style in the place, talk about everything from bank rates to oat bran, and then finally get down to their true purpose, the T-straps they came in for in the first place.

"Maggie, dear—" Here it comes.

"Yes, Sonia dear—"

"Be serious, Maggie. What I have to ask you is serious."

"I'm serious."

"What did Dan tell you about his trip to California?"

"Not much. Only that he was going to check out a few new tours and things in San Francisco and maybe drive down to LA."

"That's all he said? Nothing more?"

She was insinuating something, making mischief, the same as she was with that cute little story about her manicurist seeing Dan in Central Park. The conversation has started to bore me. "Sonia, dear, I think I should tell you Dan's given up jogging. He's hung up his Reeboks. We've bought an Exercycle."

"Maggie, dear. I'm thinking only of you. Believe me."

"I believe you."

"Does the name Liza mean anything to you?"

"You mean he's having an affair with Liza Minnelli?"

"I give up."

"I wish you would, Sonia. I'm getting tired of your insinuations. You say you're trying to save our marriage? That's not how it looks to me. I'm really not interested in discussing this further. I've got a million things to do."

"It's your funeral, Maggie. But don't ever say I didn't warn you. The facts are these. Liza's model agency is one of Dan's new accounts. Liza is in the San Francisco area on a location shoot all this week. Now Dan has flown out to San Francisco for no good reason. In my book, one and one makes two."

"I hate to spoil your fun, Sonia, but Daniel begged me to go with him, but our regular sitter is away. In fact, if she gets back in time, I'm flying out to join him."

"If that's your story, then lots of luck."

It's the only story I have. I keep going over my conversation with Daniel. I was the one who suggested he get away for a few days, wasn't I? So he couldn't have planned to meet this Liza, could he? A coincidence is all it is. Sonia's dirty mind jumping to conclusions. Trying to save our marriage!

Trying to make trouble is more like it. All that drivel about wanting to prevent a divorce for her own selfish reasons. I can see now what she's really trying to do. If Daniel and I divorced, he'd have more time for business, more time to bring in the bucks for her.

I'll be glad when Daniel gets back. He said he wasn't sure where he'd be staying but I wasn't to worry, he'd call me. He hasn't called so far. He flew out last night and probably didn't want to wake us up. It's ten in the morning now, three hours earlier in San Francisco. Any moment the phone will ring.

Liza

It was early. I ordered room service—papaya and sliced oranges. Might as well live it up. In the early morning hours, the Bay is a Japanese print, the mist striated with wisps of melon pink, the bridge itself a shimmering blur. The plane didn't leave until two. The gang could take care of itself. I would go for a walk.

A knock on the door announced breakfast.

"Come on in." I love room service—the sound of the keys in the lock, the sight of the liveried waiter wheeling in the thick padded table covered in crisp linen with heated plates, enough cutlery for twelve courses, a single rose in a bud vase, and the morning newspaper so pristine it must have been ironed. I love the little crinkled paper shower cap on the water glass to protect it on the long journey upstairs from the kitchens, and the tiny jars of Tiptree jam that I purloin both for their contents and for later use as travel containers for toiletries.

I was in my robe, brushing my hair at the bedroom mirror and languidly indicating the window. "Put it over there, please." What luxury. I could really live in a hotel. The waiter nodded, fussed with the placement of the chair, and approached me with the check for my signature.

"I'd rather put it over here." He moved up close behind me, pulled back the collar of my robe, and kissed the nape of my neck.

Daniel.

How did he manage such a thing? Later, he told me that the hotel management knew him from years of doing business and were delighted to help him play this harmless little joke on an old friend.

"What if I had a man in my room?"

He took the hairbrush out of my hand and placed my arms around his neck, opening my robe in order to pull me close. "You have a man in your room. A man who's flown three thousand miles to tell you he loves you and wants you and won't take no for an answer."

"You're only making things worse."

"No, I'm making things better, for both of us, Liza. Listen to me. We've got a lot of talking to do."

"Talk fast. My plane leaves at two."

The others were leaving at two. I was spending the next three days with him—no argument, he was the travel agent, wasn't he? He'd made all the arrangements to drive down the Pacific Coast Highway to Los Angeles and catch a plane back home from there. "Steinbeck country, I know how much you love Steinbeck, the Monterey Peninsula, Big Sur, the Spanish missions, San Simeon. Three glorious days—and four glorious nights—all by ourselves, just the two of us. I have even managed to rent a red Trans-Am."

Get it while you ca-annnn. There was the ghost of Janis Joplin again, sitting on my shoulder, singing in my ear. There was Dan holding me and caressing me and making me feel loved and appreciated after a job well done. The weekend was ahead. There was nothing waiting for me in New York except my empty apartment and a blind date with a recently widowered broker with three children who'd been given my number by someone I scarcely know.

I repeated to myself the litany of the self-deluded: Life was short. I deserved a little happiness. The plane could crash. I could be dead tomorrow. If I said no, I'd be sorry. Three little days wouldn't hurt anybody.

We made love until the mist cleared and shared my breakfast at the window, incredulous at the sight of San Francisco Bay and the graceful wonder of the bridge gleaming in the sunshine. I told Athena my change of plan and that I would see her next week. She sounded hurt, but I couldn't help that. She had looked forward to the trip east, she had lots of things to discuss with me. But I'm not her baby-sitter. I told her to be a good girl, that a car would be waiting at Kennedy to take her home, and that I had important business in Los Angeles.

"On the weekend?"

Screw her, screw her mother; they had just earned a fast twenty grand for standing around and pouting into the camera, and this was the last El Cheapo job. From now on, no more catalog work for Athena. From now on, only major bucks for exclusive print ads and commercials and who-knows-what lay ahead.

"Movie people, Athena. Movie people I've been talking to about a vehicle for you."

A Trans-Am is more than a convertible. It heightens the senses. It's like the difference between champagne in fluted Waterford and the same champagne in a plastic cup. As we roared up and down the streets of San Francisco toward the coast road, people grinned at us and some waved. A boy yelled, "Right on!" We were as romantically exciting to the world as we were to ourselves. It was savor-time again, living for the moment. With the sharp salt air battering my face and blowing my hair to smithereens, and Dan beside me, laughing and singing and telling me how happy he was, I knew it was worth it, whatever happened. There were no guarantees. Newlyweds died in car wrecks. Cancer claims millions. Let's hear it again from Janis: *Get it while you can.*

At Cannery Row, I hugged the bust of John Steinbeck in a rush of silliness and thanked him for his books.

"You're out of your mind. I'm in love with a crazy lady!"

I was out of my mind. I was crazy with pleasure after all the weeks of loneliness and grief. At Big Sur, we stood on a bluff high above the Pacific as the sun set in the west, purple crimson flames across the far horizon, millions of miles wide as far as the eyes could see, nature at its most glorious.

"I'm asking you to marry me, Liza."

The moment was so exquisite, I didn't want to spoil it by mentioning one small problem: he was already married.

He sensed my reaction. "Please, darling, listen to me. These last weeks have been hell. I've thought the whole thing through. I can't live without you. The minute I get back, I'm asking Maggie for a divorce."

Daniel

I'm one lucky bastard. I don't deserve such complete happiness. I've never felt such oneness with another human being. We're totally in tune. We finish each other's sentences. We laugh—and cry—at the same things. I can say things to her I've never said to a living soul without being embarrassed or shy. I know she's not going to sneer or think I'm some kind of perverted sex maniac. She says it's the same for her, that she's never trusted anyone the way she trusts me, that she's never gone as far in exploring her sexuality as we have together.

The trip down the coast has been a series of small and amazing adventures. The scenery itself can blow your mind. I have my trusty camera, and I've been taking pictures like it was going out of style, like I want every image of Liza I can capture. Liza with her arms around Steinbeck. Liza peeing behind some bushes—all you can see is her face grinning with relief. Liza running on the beach. Liza staring up at one of William Randolph Hearst's nude statues at San Simeon. Liza asleep on the bed after we made love.

I get a kick out of taking her picture. She says it's dangerous, what if Maggie sees them, then what? She reminds me of the ones I took at her apartment. What happened to them? She knew it wasn't cool posing for them. She hoped I hadn't left them where Maggie or the children might stumble across them.

As a matter of fact, I had forgotten all about them. They were still at the drugstore, waiting to be picked up. I had thought of exposing the film, throwing the whole damn thing away, until I remembered that Sandi and Jennifer were on the first few frames, baking cookies and up to their ears in flour. I didn't want to lose those.

Tonight's our last night together. This afternoon, we stopped at a roadside shopping mart and bought T-shirts we won't ever wear and postcards we won't ever send. While she was trying to decide on a scarf for Myrna, I slipped over to a jewelry stand and bought her a silver ring set with tiny "rubies" around a large zircon "diamond." At the nearby cafe, a couple at the next table asked if we were on our honeymoon. I laughed. Liza blushed. We held hands and kissed so as not to disappoint them.

I knew I should be calling home. It was just a matter of finding the right moment. I didn't want to break the spell. I wanted this trip to last forever, to keep driving until we hit Mexico, Central America, Venezuela, Peru—all the way to Tierra del Fuego, and then all the way back again.

Over dinner, I gave her the ring. "Will you marry me?" She held out her left hand. I slipped it on her third finger, a perfect fit. She pressed the ring to her lips and closed her eyes in a vain attempt to stop the tears. Taking my hand in hers, she whispered, "Yes, Daniel. I will."

I know this is right. We belong together. I don't want to cause unhappiness, but it can't be helped. Maggie will find someone else. I've seen the way men look at her. The girls will be upset, but they'll be better off in the long run. I can't be a good father if I'm miserable, like I was when I bit Jennifer's head off about that punk outfit. Calling my own daugther a whore, I should have been horsewhipped for that. It'll take time, I know, but the kids will grow to love Liza, too, I'm sure of it. And if I'm happy, I'll be able to do that much more for them.

When we get to Los Angeles, the first thing I'm going to do is call them and ask them what they want Daddy to bring them from California.

Liza

Usually I feel intimidated by Beverly Hills. I feel fat. I feel old. I feel ugly. My clothes are grotesquely and totally wrong. My hair goes beserk and looks like a ten-dollar wig that I've put on backwards. My two-hundred-dollar Saks Fifth Avenue sunglasses look as if I bought them from a Nigerian street vendor for three dollars. The sleek, sassy appearance I can put together in ten seconds flat in New York falls apart on me the minute I hit southern California. Worst of all, my skin refuses to tan. No matter what I do—lotions, creams, oils—my legs attract the sun in splotches like camouflage fabric, my nose looks like steak tartare, and when I try a jovial smile, my lips crack like the San Andreas fault.

Rodeo Drive and its surrounds remind me of a gigantic film set for an old-time movie musical, the storefronts a Potemkin village of mythic splendor peopled by extras of mind-blowing perfection who are bused in each day to dress the set. In New York I'm in pretty good shape, flat in the gut and butt, firm enough to appear nude in the right circumstances. Here I look like the "Before" photo in a health club ad. I tell myself these bronzed goddesses are mutants from a far planet—no pores, no pimples and, most suspiciously, they don't sweat—which has never eased the stabbing envy of heart and soul at the sight of a sun-kissed couple parked in a drophead Mercedes, bare legs draped over the polished doors, munching enchiladas and wiping their greasy hands on the crimson glove-leather seats. The atmosphere fries your brains if you're not careful.

This time was different. This time, riding beside Dan with fingers entwined in the serenity of the sexually appeased, I didn't feel the slightest twinge of deprivation. As we pulled into the Beverly Wilshire, I was happy; my only sense of inadequacy would have been in describing my happiness. How banal can you get? Happiness is beyond banality and beyond description. It immunizes you from envy. Waiting to register, I caught a glimpse of myself in a mirror. I looked fabulous, soft and earthy, with an organic kind of beauty that did not depend on designer clothes and a Fifty-seventh Street haircut.

Once in our suite, we tested the king-size bed and decided to take showers, make love, and then figure out what to do for lunch.

"You don't mind if I call home, do you?" Dan asked.

"It's okay. I'll go into the other room."

"No, Liza. Stay right here. You're part of my life now. I don't want to hide anything from you." He smiled with paternal anticipation. "I know there's going to be a period of adjustment, but I can't wait for you to meet the girls."

I could hear a click and a muffled voice.

"They'll be having breakfast. Maggie? Good morning. How're you all doing?"

Regardless of his wishes, I felt awkward being right there, as if I were somehow gloating while he called his wife. She was not my enemy. I did not feel smug or triumphant. I might be the Other Woman, but I could honestly say I did not steal her husband. I did not wreck her home. I was the one who called off the affair. He was the one who followed me to California. It was his decision to leave her and marry me.

"My God! Oh, my God!" Dan staggered against the table, knocking over the lamp. "What hospital? When? For God's sake, Maggie, tell me the truth. She's not dead, is she? Tell me she's not dead. You swear? I'll be there as fast as I can. I'm leaving right now for the airport."

He looked as if he'd been hit by a truck but hadn't fallen down, his face a melting latex mask, the flesh sagging and shapeless, his eyes demented. It was Jennifer. "Day before yesterday, an emergency appendectomy. She was in pain, but she was afraid to say anything because Maggie had caught her eating a frozen pizza without defrosting it and she thought the bellyache was from that. Peritonitis may have set in. She's in intensive care. I should have been there."

"Oh, darling. I'm so sorry." I tried to put my arm around him. He pushed me away so savagely, I tripped and fell to the floor.

"It's all your fault!" He stabbed his pointed finger in my face. For a terrible moment, I thought he was going to kick me. I held my tongue. It did not seem appropriate to point out that he had neglected to call home. He was in such agony, I wasn't going to argue. If it made it easier to blame me, he could blame me. We could discuss it later.

"Do you want me to drive you to the airport?"

There was no need to pack. We had not had a chance to unpack.

"I'll catch a cab."

He couldn't look at me. He couldn't kiss me goodbye. He was in such a frenzy to leave, he left the door of the suite open as he ran down the corridor like the place was on fire.

So there I was, alone in a magnificent suite with a basket of fruit. I was in shock, like an earthquake victim engulfed in emotional rubble and wondering what to do next. I ate all the strawberries in the fruit basket and called room service for a cheese Danish and a hot chocolate. I knew I should be feeling sorry for Dan and worried about his daughter, but in my secret heart of hearts, I was angry. *Why did this have to happen to me?* I know it makes me a selfish bitch, but that's how I felt. Didn't I deserve a little happiness? Why did Jennifer have to get sick on my time with Dan? I'm ashamed of feeling this way. I'll never be able to say these things to anyone, and certainly never to Dan.

The point is he shut me out. He says he loves me, but he wouldn't let me share his pain. He wouldn't let me drive him to the airport. He wanted to get away from me as fast as he could. The man who made love to me this morning and vowed that he would love me forever and give me a child has left me without a word. Okay, so I'm not being fair. The man is hysterical with fear for his daughter's life and guilty for failing to call home.

I remember being on a seesaw as a child when, suddenly, without warning, when I was sky high, the other person got off and I crashed to the ground, the wind knocked out of me, stunned and unable to cry. That's how I feel now.

Daniel

My chest hurt. I couldn't breathe. I felt so nauseous, the driver had to get off the freeway so I could throw up. I thought I might be having a heart attack and should head for the nearest hospital instead of the airport. If it was a heart attack, it would have to wait until I got to New York, that's all there was to it.

I pulled myself together and by the time we hit LA International, I could breathe again.

"Maggie? My flight boards in ten minutes."

Sandi was on the extension, sobbing, "Where were you, Daddy? We couldn't find you!"

"Don't worry, Punkin'. Daddy'll be right there. Promise. Take care of Mommy for me, okay?"

After a double bourbon, I could phone the Beverly Wilshire Hotel. Mercifully, she was still there.

"Liza?"

"Dan. My God. Are you okay?"

"Please, darling. Forgive me. I'm sorry for what I said. Of course it's not your fault. I don't know what made me say that. Will you forgive me?"

"Oh, Dan. I was so worried. Of course you're upset. It's your daughter, your baby." She choked up and couldn't speak, reminding me how sad she'd looked the night she told me about the baby she'd lost. "I'm sorry, Dan. I should be cheering you up instead of falling apart. It's your little girl, not mine."

"You'll have your own little girl one day. Our little girl, Liza, just like we said. Remember?"

"Promise?"

"Promise."

She tried to make a joke about hiring a toy-boy to replace me for the rest of her stay.

I tried to respond in kind: "You'll need at least ten to replace me." But the words turned to sand in my mouth.

I could hear my flight being called.

"Take care of yourself, Liza."

"You, too."

"And, Liza—"

"I'm here."

"You know I didn't mean what I said."

"I know."

"Remember one thing—"

"I remember everything, Dan, every single wonderful thing—"

"I love you, right?"

"I love you, too."

"And we're going to be married, right?"

"Right."

"Keep the thought."

Liza

Thank God for friends, Peggy in particular. A Holmby Hills blonde with perfect nails and a deceptively laid-back air, she's the wisest woman I know. Although she holds several degrees in literature and fine arts, her philosophy of life is generally expressed in a breathless Marilyn Monroe whisper—"Cut the crap."

I am in a state of aftershock and suffering from a bad case of post-parting down-and-dirty my-man's-gone-now blues. Over an avocado and bean sprouts salad, Peggy says, "I have two words of advice. Get out. Get out before they carry you out or lay you out for burial."

"But he really loves me and wants to marry me."

"Sure he does."

"He just called me from the airport. His daughter's in intensive care and he still made time to call me."

"What else is there to do at an airport?"

"Peggy—I was bringing him to meet you, to get your expert opinion. I swear to you, he's the best thing that ever happened to me."

"Cut the crap, Liza. For a smart lady, you've got rocks in your head. The man is married."

"He's getting a divorce."

"That's what you say."

"That's what he says."

"That's what they all say, Liza. Take it from me, there are millions of Daniels around. They grow on Daniel trees. It's Adam and Eve in reverse. Eve tempted Adam with the apple. The Daniel tree grows married men for the sole purpose of tempting single women—*naive* single women—to sin and shame."

"Dan isn't like that."

"Of course not."

"The time we broke up, he was miserable."

"Of course he was miserable. He doesn't just want to have his cake and eat it, he wants the whole damned bakery."

"It's not like that. We love each other. The last few days have been the most wonderful, the most ecstatic—"

"Please, Liza, spare me." She sprinkles jalapeno flakes on her skim milk yogurt. "You're suffering from erotic meltdown. I don't want to see you hurt. I'll bet you a hundred dollars he never leaves his wife. Make it a thousand. Make it a million. There'll always be an excuse, count on it. Right now it's his kid's appendicitis. Next time, it'll be something else, count on it."

"But Jennifer's in the hospital, for God's sake, in intensive care. How can he ask for a divorce at a time like this?"

Peggy gazed at me with affectionate pity. "See what I mean? Cut the crap, Liza. Run, do not walk, to the nearest exit."

Maggie

I never thought myself capable of murder. Now I know that I am. If I could kill Daniel and get away with it, I would.

Daniel

Maggie is waiting for me at the airport, her face a stony mask. Without makeup and with her hair scraped back tighter than usual, she looks like the daguerreotype of her great-grandmother, who settled the Arizona territory.

"Maggie—"

Her eyes are cold, full of accusation mixed with contempt. *Jennifer,* my God! She can't be dead, can she? An appendectomy is a simple operation these days, like having a tooth pulled. Everyone always says so.

"Maggie, *please*—tell me how she is."

"The car's outside."

Is my child dead or alive? The mother of our child can no longer contain her disgust. She turns from me and leads the way to the parking lot. When I take her arm, she stops and removes my hand with two fingers, as if it were a dead rat. I am so frightened and ashamed, I feel faint. Jennifer, my little girl. Why wasn't I here? All the way across the country, all I could think was, *Why didn't I know?* Why didn't I feel something was wrong? Where was my mental telepathy?

My sweet little girl at death's door, and what was I doing? I was proving what a big man I am, what a hot lover, what a poor excuse for a human being. I should be horsewhipped or worse. Instead, I was tooling down the Pacific Coast Highway in a convertible with my hand under Liza's skirt like some lecherous asshole. What in God's name did I think I was doing? Jennifer's under the knife and I'm humping on a California beach.

"Please, Maggie, don't do this to me. You've got every right to punish me. I'm punishing myself. I'll never forgive myself. Tell me, please, for God's sake, tell me how she is."

"How do you think she is?"

Where is the car taking us? To the hospital, to the funeral home? "Maggie, *please—*"

She sighs deeply, as if bored, and half turns her back on me in order to look out the window. "She'll be fine," she says, almost to herself.

"She's *what?* For God's sake, Maggie. The traffic and everything. Speak up. I can't hear you."

She turns slowly toward me, puts her lips close to my ear, and screams, "She's fine! Can you hear me now?" Her outburst breaks the tension. In her normal, if frigid, tone of voice, she says things had been touch and go. Dr. Minkow had packed Jennifer in ice and gotten her into surgery before the appendix erupted. It turned out to be a textbook operation. That had been two days ago, at about the time Liza and I were visiting Mr. Hearst's love nest at San Simeon.

"How's she making out?"

"Our daughter is young, strong, and healthy. By last night, she could sit up in bed and dangle her feet."

"Thank God. Will I be able to see her?"

She again looks at me with revulsion. I am a cockroach with

the temerity to invade her clean kitchen floor. "You will unless you're not planning to join us at home."

"She's home? Why didn't you tell me?"

"I didn't think you were interested."

At that I fall apart with the dry heaves. It would serve me right to have a heart attack. Maggie takes minimal pity on me. She pats my arm like a social worker in a communicable disease ward. "Pull yourself together. Dr. Minkow said the only reason he discharged her so soon is because I'm a full-time mother. Otherwise, she'd still be in the hospital."

"So who's with her now? Why did you leave her alone? I could have gotten a cab by myself. What if she needs something? What if she breaks her stitches?"

Despite her determination to break my ass, Maggie smiles. "Wait till you see Sandi, a regular little Florence Nightingale, or maybe Hawkeye's more like it. She told Dr. Minkow she's planning to go to medical school, the little flirt. He said he thought her competent enough to leave in charge while I came to pick you up—and told me privately he would drop back in a half hour just to be sure."

I am trembling with thankfulness and relief. God has taught me a lesson and given me another chance. If Jennifer had died, they'd have said it was a ruptured appendix. I know differently. It was my fault. God has forgiven me. More than anything, I want Maggie to do the same, though I don't see how she can. I've taken her for granted—her beauty, her values, her talents as a homemaker, our children, her making it all seem so easy, no sweat, smooth as silk, a piece of cake.

By the time we get home, both girls are asleep. Sandi is in her Bambi sleeping bag on the floor beside her sister, a sentinel on guard. Sandi's favorite Hug bear, which she has never so much as permitted her older sister to touch, is nestled in Jennifer's arms. My heart swells to bursting; such warm and loving girls, and all because of their mother. I feel humbled and less worthy than ever.

"Maggie—" We're sitting at the kitchen table, but with the formality of strangers.

"Would you like some coffee? A sandwich?"

"There's something I have to tell you." The guilty man wants to make a clean breast of things. She knows something's been going on. I want to tell her what happened—everything, the full story—and beg her forgiveness.

"You don't have to tell me." The look of contempt returns. "I know."

When the corner drugstore delivered Jennifer's medication, they thoughtfully included the pictures I had left for development a few weeks back. No question about it, I really was asking to be caught. There is Liza in her apartment in living, loving color, lying back on the mountain of pillows like a sultan's favorite. There is Liza mugging for the camera in the zany way all lovers do—pornographic, no; but intimate, yes.

I look over the prints with Maggie's eyes and cringe. Liza wearing a bath towel. Me in the same bath towel, wearing a baseball cap. Liza in bed, reading *The Joy of Sex* upside down. Me in bed with my baseball cap still on, reading *Business Week* with a flashlight. We had found other things to do with that flashlight. Thank God we had not photographed that. The last few were of Liza's face in full-frame close-up, eyes closed, lips moist and pursed for a kiss.

I remember the day I dropped them off, and afterwards thinking it was a stupid and dangerous thing to do. I should have taken them somewhere else just to be sure. On the other hand, I was the one who took care of photographs, wasn't I? The receipt was in my billfold. Who could have predicted what happened? That's what you get with a friendly neighborhood drugstore.

"I'm—what can I say, Maggie? I'm mortified—I can't stand to hurt you like this—I'm sorry—"

She is watching my face as if I'm speaking a foreign language. She is perplexed and trying to understand. I am on trial for my life, and the evidence against me is overwhelming. I have no defense. I have caused pain and suffering, committed crimes against my wife and children. No plea bargain is possible. She is judge and jury. The verdict is up to her.

"I'm sorry, too."

Then it's settled. She wants me to leave. I can't blame her. She must hate the very sight of me. I'm so nervous, I start to laugh, a hideous hyena laugh. The more I try to stop, the louder and more hysterical I get, until the laughter turns to spasmodic sobs, ripping my throat and chest like serrated knives. Maggie watches me as if waiting to see what happens next. Will I go into convulsions? With enormous effort, I calm myself down. Maggie pours me a Courvoisier.

"I get the message. It's okay. I'm leaving." I can't stay here. It's making her puke just to look at me. A hotel? I can't remember the last time I stayed in a New York hotel. I've always had a home and a wife waiting for me. Not that I'll have a problem finding a room. I am, after all, in the travel business.

I knock back the brandy and head for the front door, Maggie following me as if to make sure I leave.

"Daniel."

My hand is on the doorknob. I can feel her close behind me. We are in darkness, except for the tiny pinpoint of light coming through the peephole Maggie always used for a secret look at me while I waited for the elevator. It always tickled me that she did it, but I never let on.

"You can watch me through the peephole. Make sure I've gone."

"You knew I was watching you?" She's against me now, her breath on the back of my neck in the darkness. "Why didn't you tell me?"

I can't handle the repartee. I have to get the hell out of here before I make a jerk of myself again. If I'm not careful, I'll be blubbering like an old man. I turn the doorknob. Her hand covers mine. "I want to know, Daniel. Why didn't you tell me?"

About knowing she watched me through the peephole? Or about Liza? I choose the former. "Because it made me feel so good, so proud. Because it made me so happy to know the woman I loved also loved me, loved me so much she couldn't keep her eyes off me. It probably sounds weird, but I would stand there feeling your eyes on me and it sent shivers up and down my spine."

"I'm watching you now, Daniel, close up. How do you feel now?"

She takes her hand off mine. I can turn the doorknob and go. I sag against the door like a bag of laundry. I have forgotten how physically strong Maggie is. She props me up by my elbows and spins me around. Our bodies are pasted together. The pinpoint of light illuminates her eyes.

"I'll repeat the question, Daniel. How do you feel now?"

I collapse against her, my face buried in her neck. "Please take me back."

She takes me to our bed and holds me in her arms as if I were the prodigal son. She says she can understand why women throw themselves at me. She says she can understand why I was attracted to Liza. She wants our marriage to work and she is willing to work at it if I am willing to work at it, too. She says she understands if I don't want to make love. She is stroking my hair and rubbing my neck the way she does to the girls when they are fretful, and soon I'm floating in a zone of peaceful surrender.

A voice inside me reminds me not to call her Liza by mistake. I will have to forget Liza. My wife, my children, my home are the most important things in my life. I will miss Liza. I will think of Liza. But I will never see her again.

Maggie

I ripped the pictures up and was about to throw them in the garbage, and then I changed my mind. I might need them for something, I'm not sure what, evidence or whatever. I've been foolish, but I'm going to stop being a fool. It's time to think of Number One; I'm getting a safe-deposit box as a start. That was Helen's idea, that I should start accumulating a little stash of my own; you never know what's down the road.

It took me half the morning to stick those pictures back together. It strengthened my resolve to be prepared for next time—if there is a next time. There's something very satisfying about your own safe-deposit box. It belongs to you and you alone, no spouse. Where the application asks for next of kin, I put Helen's name. This is something I want to keep separate from Dan, a place for those pictures and for the cash I'm planning to save from my housekeeping money.

My getaway money after I kill him. I could change my name, wear a wig, and disappear; start again somewhere else. Who'd have thought it of me? "Mild-Mannered Mom Murders Husband." They'd blame it on hormonal imbalance or an old-fashioned nervous breakdown. "Neighbors and Friends Surprised." Why would they be surprised? Every day's news has some lunatic killer described as quiet, pleasant, and friendly.

That's me, but add vigilant. I can't run away and start again. I'm too old, I'm too shy, I'm too hurt and insecure; and anyway, why should I be the one to run, to give up my children and my home? It's *my* home, my children's home; he uses it as a hotel. Now that I've calmed down, I'm wondering what it would be like if I'd thrown him the hell out. Other women do fine in a divorce—never happier. They redecorate the apartment, have dinner parties, take a young lover. Collect the alimony. Get a job. Join Parents Without Partners.

Who am I kidding? I'm going to fight for my marriage. I've got the upper hand now, and I intend to keep it. Dan slept in my arms like a baby. That's when I nearly smothered him with a pillow. *Bastard.* That look on his face is even worse. *Please forgive me, I'm sorry, I'll make it up to you.* Jennifer really scared him. He's convinced his daughter nearly died to teach him a lesson.

We've agreed to keep this Liza episode to ourselves. Dan was in California, as we all know. He rushed home when he heard about Jennifer. He's horrified when I tell him about Sonia's phone call to me. "Does the name Liza mean anything to you?"

"She asked you that?"

"I told her it was my idea for you to get away. And that you had asked me to join you, so she was completely off base about this Liza."

He had the grace to look sheepish. "What is she, a detective? Wait till I get my hands on her."

"No, Dan, don't. Let her simmer in her own juice. If she

mentions Liza and California, say something about checking with her to be sure the arrangements went as planned. She is a client, after all."

From habit, I walked him to the door and watched him through the peephole. He looked tanned and handsome but older, beaten down. On impulse, I phoned Sonia to say he was on his way. "He's still a nervous wreck over Jennifer. He tossed and turned all night. He kept tiptoeing into her room to be sure she was all right. He needs all the tender loving care we can give him, Sonia. I know I can count on you."

This was the first time in my life that I'd tried to manipulate anyone. Poor Dan, Sonia said, of course I could count on her; we were family, weren't we? Jerking her around had turned out to be depressingly easy.

I do not think she will confront him with Liza. What she doesn't know won't hurt her, or us. I'd love to have seen her face if I'd shown her those pictures. Those *pictures!* They're in the safe-deposit box if I need them. I'd better put them right out of my mind. They remind me of my honeymoon.

Someone had given us a Polaroid camera as a wedding present. Dan could not stop taking pictures of me . . . "Hold it, don't move, just like that, perfect!" We were so happy, so much in love; I was his, I had pledged my life to him, I would do anything he asked of me—except for one thing.

He asked me to pose for him in a certain way, and I refused. "It's all right, darling," he said. I can still see his face and hear his voice. "We're married, we love each other." He loved every inch of me, didn't he? He would never hurt me, would he? All he wanted to do was take the picture; we could look at it together and tear it to shreds. Nobody would ever see it but us.

That was the point. *I* would see it. I ran to the bathroom and was sick.

Dan never again made that particular suggestion. He has never mentioned the incident, and neither have I.

Liza

Four days and not a word. I'm worried sick. The poor guy, he must be camping out at the hospital, out of his mind with anxiety. Maybe Jennifer's dead. Kids die, too. If she is dead, how would I know? If only I could be with him to help him through this thing. He must be going crazy. I'm sure he wants to call me, but how can he, with Maggie right there and Sandi, too. God! If I knew what hospital she was in, I could send something—anonymously, of course.

What am I talking about? It's none of my business. She's not my child. If I keep this up, they'll take me away to the rubber room. But I've got to find out what's happening. I guess I could call his office. After all, I am a client. I've had Myrna make the arrangements up to now to avoid complications. I've had no cozy chats that could be overheard. Myrna, of course, doesn't know about California. There's no reason why I can't ask her to call Dan's office and find out when he's expected back.

"He's been back for the last three days," she says. He's out on a call and is expected back any minute. Do I want to leave my name?

No, I manage to say, it's all right. No message.

I knew it all along, of course. No matter what's going on, if a man cares, he'll find a way to call. Now I know. All I can do is count myself lucky that it happened when it did. I could have let it go on for months. I could have gotten pregnant. I could have been making plans. Jennifer did me a big favor. It's over.

Forget it. If my father was Don Corleone, I'd have his knees broken. Look on the bright side: the phones are ringing off the hook, the California session was a smash, the client sent roses and is talking about an invitation to serve on their corporate board.

Less bright is the fence-mending I still have to do with Irini. When I got back, there must have been fifty messages from her on my machine at home as well as at the office. She must speak to me. She had to speak to me. It was urgent that we speak.

Myrna was trying to be witty. "I get the impression she wants to speak to you."

It was too important to discuss on the phone; she had to see me in person. "Alone." Before California, this would have sounded ominous. But after what I've just been through with Dirty Dan, I can handle anything. Today's the day. She's due here any minute. Whatever she has in mind, I'm ready.

"There's a man on the phone. Refuses to give his name. Says it's personal." Myrna is thrilled by this sort of thing.

Dan? God! "Tell him I'm not here."

"I already said you were."

I am an ice cream cone in the sun; a melting, sticky mess.

"Hello—"

It is not Dan. It is the Englishman I met on the plane. Would I care to dine? The rule is, if you fall off the horse, get right back on or you'll never ride again. I tell him to pick me up at seven. God save the Queen and the British Empire.

I am no longer upset. I refuse to be upset. Daniel is a psychopath, and that's all there is to it. He looks normal. He acts normal. He's a Brooks Brothers Bluebeard. He hates women, but he craves our bodies. He gets his rocks off, and then he wants to destroy the woman who holds sexual power over him. The old madonna-whore complex. Maggie's the madonna he goes running back to, saying *mea culpa, mea culpa,* Danny baby has sinned with Liza and now he's tired and doesn't want to play.

At this point, I'm willing to bet Jennifer wasn't sick at all. He made the whole thing up. He wanted to cut and run. He found a patsy for company. I should really send him a bill for services rendered, a detailed account.

Enough already. In a week I won't remember his face. In a month, I won't even remember his name. The first step is to change travel agents.

Myrna has just announced Irini, and has added that the Penrose family have confirmed their afternoon appointment. I may have stumbled on a blockbuster, a black family that combines the Jackson Five and the Huxtables—gorgeous, talented, and including a twelve-year-old girl who looks like a Watusi princess. I found them poolside at the Wilshire. They'd been seeing agents and getting nowhere. I gave them my card and told them to look me up if they got to New York.

Serendipity is a two-faced goddess. She bumps you into Daniel in Central Park and nearly wrecks your life. Then, to make up for it, she takes you for a swim at the Beverly Wilshire pool.

Irini comes right to the point. Johnny Casablancas wants to manage Athena's career. He has the greatest respect for what I've done, but I haven't the international contacts and resources that he has. With him, Athena can be an international superstar. Modeling is just the beginning. My Revlon deal is peanuts; well, maybe not exactly peanuts, but very little compared to what lies ahead. Movies, for instance. Rock and roll. Las Vegas.

"She can't act, Irini. She can barely speak."

"He'll get lessons for her. Brooke Shields can't act, either."

"She's been famous since she was a baby. America loves her. It doesn't matter if she can act. Athena is just beginning."

Irini is not listening. "A recording contract. He'll get a backup group, music videos."

"Can Athena sing?"

"It doesn't matter. It's all visual. When you hear rock and roll, can you tell who's singing?"

"I'm not a teenager. What the hell is this, Irini? Are you giving me the ax, or is this a negotiation? I really don't have time for this shit."

"You don't have to use vulgar language, Liza. I am a lady."

"Shit is not vulgar. Shit is healthy. If you don't shit, you die. What you've been saying is vulgar. You and your daughter have signed a contract with me. If you want to walk away, I can't stop you. I can sic my lawyer on you. I can demand that you fulfill the Revlon contract—you'd be crazy not to. I could further demand a split commission from Casablancas for the duration of our contract. All this is time-consuming and expensive. But I can't stop you from leaving, if that's what you want to do. So make up your mind. I'm running late as it is."

At this point, I really don't care what she decides. She can take the contract and stuff it up her kazoo. There are people who do things and people who complicate things. I'm in the wrong line of work. I may throw everything up and join the Peace Corps.

"Liza, darling—don't be angry."

"I'm not angry. I'm fed up."

"You're angry and you're right to be angry."

It takes a few more rounds of byzantine bullshit to work

things out. They will decline Johnny's flattering offer. I will decrease my commission by a half percent and also pay Irini a monthly fee as a consultant.

I manage to forget about Dan until I get home. Then he's all around me. I can feel him. I can smell him. I can taste him. It's a good thing I've made a date with the Englishman. He arrives with a bottle of Stolichnaya and a package of bacon rinds. "Change of plan," he says looking around my living room with evident satisfaction. "Thought we'd stay in and get acquainted."

One of those. That's all I need. I figure one drink and I'll throw him out. In the time it takes me to get ice and glasses from the kitchen, he's stripped and is displaying himself on the couch.

"I see you wear a bikini," I say.

"Clever girl. I knew we'd get on. Come to me at once."

A Monty Python reject. That's all I need. Another time, I'd find it funny. Tonight, I really don't need this. I didn't really expect much—a nice dinner maybe, a friendly grope in the cab, and maybe even an overnight cuddle, if it worked out and could take my mind off Dan.

"Out! I'll give you two minutes. I'm a black belt and I'll break you in half if you say one more word."

He takes the vodka with him but leaves the bacon rinds. I wait at the window for him to emerge from under the awning and hurl the package down at him. It lands on top of the awning. Oh, Liza, you can't do anything right.

The phone rings. *Dan!* My mother says Mark wants to know if I'm still running around with that married man.

"How many times do I have to tell you, it's none of his business?"

"He and Tiffany have broken up."

"What do you want me to do? Light candles?"

"He wants to call you."

"Then why doesn't he call me, Mother dear? Doesn't he know how to operate a telephone?"

"He's afraid you'll bite his head off."

He's right.

The night is young; it's the perfect opportunity to straighten up the apartment. I haven't really unpacked since I got back. Mail and magazines are piled on the table. My dry cleaning is still draped over a chair the way it was delivered. I'm too restless. I can't concentrate. I open a can of pork and beans to eat cold with a glass of red wine and turn on the TV. This is not my night. On every channel, they're making love. I can't stand it. They're all panting and moaning and the music is swelling behind them and I'm sitting here getting fat on baked beans. It's not fair. I want Dan. I can't let it end like this without a word or a goodbye and good luck.

I look up his name in the phone book. What if he's not listed? Why shouldn't he be listed? Who would he be hiding from, except me? Sure enough, there he is in black and white. A West Side address, of course; married men always live on the West Side. I push-button the number and wait. At last, a man answers. *Dan.*

Daniel

How could Liza do such a thing? Couldn't she understand? Jennifer nearly died. Maggie was up with her for two days straight, afraid to close her eyes in case something happened while she wasn't looking. She was a tower of strength. Sandi is still having nightmares. She wakes up in the middle of the night, screaming Jennifer's name until we all reassure her Jennifer is here, she's not dead, and she's going to be all right.

I know I should have called Liza and let her know what was happening, but I couldn't deal with it. I started to dial her number a hundred times, but I didn't know what to say—"My child nearly died, I can't marry you"? The whole thing was an aberration, my mid-life crisis, Maggie says.

Liza's a clever lady. Why wasn't she smart enough to get the message? How dare she call me at my home and upset my wife like that! I heard Maggie pick up on the extension just as Liza said, "Dan—don't do this to me. Don't just disappear without a word. Talk to me. Tell me what's going on."

All I could think to say was, "It's over, Liza."

"Is it really over, Dan?" Maggie was dressed for bed. We were both knocked out and had planned to have an early night, reading and watching TV in bed. Her bathrobe fell open, her satin nightgown a seductive change from her customary cotton T-shirt. "Prove it!"

I tried to prove it, without success. Abysmal failure is more like it. I couldn't get it up. I couldn't prove to my wife that I love her and that she is the most important woman in the world to me.

"You're still in love with her—aren't you?"

"No, Maggie, no. I love you, I swear it. I love you and only you."

I will never understand what triggers sexuality. Her humiliation. My guilt. Whatever the complex tangle of wires connecting brain and scrotum, I was able now to prove my love, to make up for her pain by giving her pleasure in every slow and generous way I could devise, attentive to every nuance of her response, encouraging her to take risks as never before.

The height of her rapture and the depth of her happiness made me humble and ashamed.

Mark

That Rosalind is too much. I may have lost a wife, but I've gained a permanent mother-in-law. She makes no bones about why she hangs onto me. The divorce was a mistake. Liza overreacted. A husband's entitled to make one little mistake. If every wife acted like Liza over one little mistake, every couple in America would be divorced.

She thinks Liza and I should get back together.

"What about that guy I saw her with? They looked pretty tight."

"He's married, and it's all your fault. You shouldn't have let her go. She still loves you, Mark. Why don't you call her?"

"Oh, sure, so she can tell me off again? No, thanks. I'm not that masochistic." I remind Rosalind that Liza called me a pusbag and threw me out, bag and baggage, all my clothes dumped out in the hall. It was all so fast. She went nuts. I had wanted to have a serious talk with her about our marriage, why it wasn't working, what we could do to save it. She was too busy to listen.

Tiffany was beside the point; she just liked the thrill of getting laid by another woman's husband. If Liza hadn't gone nuts, the whole thing would have blown over. What Liza still doesn't understand is that she painted me into a corner. I was trapped. If she hadn't tossed me out, I wouldn't have been forced to set up house with Tiffany. "It's all Liza's fault!"

Rosalind isn't letting me off the hook. Liza is still in love with me, she claims. Since I have not married Tiffany, it is clear I do not intend to marry Tiffany and that I am still in love with Liza.

"She needs you. You need her. Both of you want success. The best way to do it is as a couple. You add to her image, she adds to yours. Think about that."

I have thought about it many times, how Liza managed to fit herself into any situation—a business dinner, a weekend with clients—poised and charming, no matter how bored. Tiffany is a disaster. Smoking a few joints is okay on the weekend, but last week, she toked up during cocktails with a delegation of some potentially heavy investors from Missouri. When one of the white-haired wives mentioned the strange smell and worried that the Waldorf was on fire, Tiffany laughed so hard she got hiccups.

But if Rosalind is right, Liza had a peculiar way of showing how much she still loves me the other day. She had three calls backed up, so would I mind getting right to the point? Why was I calling? Was it the Warhol poster?

"I told you my terms," she said. "You return the Ferlinghetti, I'll give you the Warhol. It's more than fair. Now that Warhol's dead, the value has jumped."

"I've told you a million times, *A Coney Island of the Mind* is still in print. I'll buy you a new one."

"Why can't you admit you stole it?"

"Tell you what, we can discuss it over dinner."

"Make it lunch."

She was being wary. Not dinner. Lunch. Smart move. Dinner can get complicated. That throaty voice reminded me how much I've missed her and how excruciatingly bored I am with Tiffany and her earphones and the sex toys and the goddam mousse all over the sheets. A woman's hair should feel like hair, soft and thick like Liza's, not like Naugahyde.

Liza and I have never really talked since the divorce. It's strange to be meeting an ex-wife for lunch. I wish she would shut up about the Ferlinghetti. I didn't steal it. I do not have it. I do remember reading it aloud, and how she always liked the part about a rebirth of wonder.

Daniel

Last night Maggie walked into the bedroom just as I slammed down the phone. "Don't try to fool me. You're talking to her!"

She grabbed the phone off the night table and tried to brain me with it. I struggled with her and tried to explain it was Sonia I was calling. Sonia's line was busy, as usual. She refuses to get a second line. I must have dialed her number fifty times before I hung up in exasperation.

"Maggie, please—"

"Don't 'Maggie, please' me!"

She let me take the phone.

As quietly as I could, I sat her down on the bed. "You've been drinking, haven't you?"

"What else have I got?" Her voice rose in a serrating wail.

"Answer that, what else have I got? My kids don't need me anymore. My husband doesn't want me anymore. I applied for three jobs and they said I'm too old!" She swung at me, missed, and fell back on the bed.

"Maggie, please—the girls!"

Jennifer was spending the night across the hall with her best friend, Beth. Sandi had been asleep the last time I checked. The racket must have awakened her. She stood in the bedroom door, looking tinier and more babyish than she had at dinner, her eyes big as saucers, her rabbit nightie on inside out as usual, her little bare feet so sweet and soft that I wanted to cup them in my hands and kiss the tiny toes.

"You're a rat!" she said and ran off to her own room.

It broke the spell. Maggie laughed. "You see, your own daughter thinks you're a rat, too."

"I'd better go in to her."

"She'll be fine."

"What about you? Will you be fine?"

"I'm sorry about that, Dan. If you must know, I thought I might be pregnant. Dr. Greene says it's too early to tell, but he doesn't think so. He thinks I may be starting the changes." Tears sluiced down her cheeks. "Don't you see? You said we'd be starting a new life together, and my life as a woman is over!"

What kind of nonsense was that? I reminded her of all the women who have babies at forty-two, who start new careers at fifty, who take up mountain climbing at seventy. "Where've you been?"

"Here!" she said bitterly. "Stuck at home with your kids. Not going off to Europe to ski. Not driving down the Pacific Coast Highway with another woman's husband."

There was no point arguing. She wouldn't—or couldn't—let it rest.

This morning, Sandi ran away from home before we got up. The doorman buzzed upstairs to tell us he had seen her around the corner, sitting on some steps, crying her eyes out. By the time I got there, she had disappeared. *Sandi!* I ran up and down the street like a madman, shouting her name, stopping people to ask if they'd seen a little girl, my little girl, until Jennifer found me. Sandi was safe at home and getting ready for school. She had returned to the apartment via the back way. The building staff love her and let her drive the freight elevator.

Why was I so upset, Jennifer wanted to know. Sandi does this all the time. She's an early riser. She likes going out by herself. Lecturing her on the dangers of deserted streets could wait for another time. What I wanted to know was, "Why were you crying, Sandi?"

She wouldn't talk to me this morning. She refuses to talk to me tonight. It's not funny when your eight-year-old daughter calls you a rat. Not funny at all.

Liza

Joke:

> WOMAN I: You look wonderful. What did you do?
> WOMAN II: I just lost 170 pounds.
> WOMAN I: How did you do it—diet?
> WOMAN II: No, I got rid of my boyfriend.

Looking at it another way, I could be really disgusting and think of him as a 170-pound tumor, poisoning my body and threatening my life. I've cut him out. The wound hurts and is healing. His asshole call this morning speeds the process.

"Liza, I don't know how to say this."

Now what? Yawn, yawn. The coward, calling me at the office. He knows there are people around and I have to be cool.

"I hope this won't hurt your business, but I can't in all conscience handle your travel arrangements anymore. I think it's best if I resign the account. If you like, I can suggest some other travel agents."

The condescending creep. What does he think we did before he came along, walk? It doesn't occur to him that I was going out of my way to give him business. And what did he do? Okay, girls, together now: he gave *me* the business.

"One more thing, Liza."

What now? He has AIDS? Not funny, bite your tongue, not funny at all. How could I even think such a thing? This conversation had gone into overtime.

"I must insist that you not call me at home, *ever,* do you understand? You upset my wife and my children. I simply won't have it."

"Well, you upset me and *I* have had it with this conversation. Goodbye, and don't you call me again without asking permission. In writing!"

In triplicate. Signed by his wife and children. And notarized. A card-carrying wimp. How could I ever have found him attractive? Or considered marrying him?

On to important matters. Myrna has circled a disquieting item on page six of the *Post:* International model emperor Johnny Casablancas, interviewed at Elaine's while dining with top Liza Central discovery Athena Georgopoulos and her ravishing mother, Irini, says he's planning to costar them in a movie remake of *Two Women,* the Carlo Ponti Oscar Award-winning drama that originally starred Sophia Loren.

I detect the fine hand of a publicist, prodded into action by

Irini. I have a feeling Casablancas will be as surprised as everyone else to read about his forthcoming film project.

Irini is one of those people who believes that everything she reads in the newspapers is true, even if her press agent gets it printed.

Instead of acting miffed, I call her and congratulate her effusively. "Sophia will be avocado green with envy."

Mark

This is a brand-new Liza. I've never seen her like this. If she was pretty when we got married, that was *girl* pretty. She's *woman* pretty now; she's beautiful—sleek, sophisticated, *powerful.* Meeting her for lunch, I feel like a kid on my first date, fumbling with my tie, patting down my hair, checking my zipper. She has me falling all over myself, the bitch.

She's making it plain that she's calling the shots. I had booked a table at the Four Seasons and had told my secretary to call her secretary with time and place. Myrna called back a while later. Liza preferred Pierre's, because today the special was *choucroute garnie.*

She keeps me waiting the ritual twenty minutes and arrives in a flurry of apologies and *bonjours.*

"Will Monsieur be joining you?" asks the maitre d'.

Not today, she says, brushing aside the very idea—the preposterous thought—as we are ushered to her favorite corner table with its commanding view of the door. Sure enough, within nanoseconds, in strolls the reason we are at Pierre's, this middle-aged man in Paul Stuart pinstripes—okay, this dynamite dude with a good tan and great teeth. He's with two other men. When the maitre d' indicates us with a Gallic shrug, Liza nearly swallows her breadstick, but nods regally. As he makes his way toward us, I realize he's the man I met her with in the park, the married man. Clothes certainly do make a difference; he looks taller and infinitely more imposing than he did that day.

Liza's a cool one. I can see she planned the whole thing. She lets him stand at our table for a good count of ten before deigning to notice him. "Oh, Dan. How nice. Say hello to Mark. Mark, Dan—but of course the two of you have met."

"You're looking well, Liza."

"Thank you. I'm feeling amazingly well."

"Well—I'd better get back to my people."

"Enjoy your lunch."

"Nice seeing you."

She takes my hand ostentatiously and looks at him as if he were blocking her view. "Yes."

I feel overwhelmed with tenderness. How dare this man take advantage of my wife? How can he know anything about the soft little kitten inside the high-power armor? I am remembering things—the way she cried the first time we made love, the way she tried to comfort me when we lost the baby.

"Liza—"

"Mark—"

"I'm serious. I want you to listen to me."

"I'm listening."

"I'm still in love with you."

She sips at her Lillet reflectively, her eyes staring into the middle distance. I know that look. The portcullis is down, shutting me out.

"Liza, you're not listening."

"I am listening. Please don't shout. This is a public place."

"I'm trying to tell you that the divorce was a mistake."

"Tiffany was the mistake."

"I know that. I knew it then. I know it now. It was a one-night stand. You made it more than that, Liza. You threw me into her arms."

"Come *on.*"

"Okay, okay. It was all my fault, I admit it. I've paid for it, you've paid for it. Why should we keep on paying? Why don't we give love another chance?"

"You mean rush right down to City Hall?"

"I mean seeing each other—slowly—getting to know each other again, getting you to trust me again—and love me again the way I love you."

"How does Tiffany feel about this?"

"We've split, dammit. You know we've split. Rosalind told you we split."

"Rosalind tells me a lot of things. She's determined to get us back together."

"So am I, Liza."

She picks up the menu and begins to read through each category, starting with *Pour Commencer.*

"Give me a break, Liza. Tiffany was a mistake. Everyone's entitled to one mistake. Can't you say something?"

Her eyes remain on the menu. "I've changed my mind about the *choucroute.* I'll just have the brook trout—and maybe a small endive and radicchio salad, dressing on the side."

She's playing with me. I don't blame her. I've hurt her, and I'll have to be patient. Rosalind says to give her a little time—"She's still carrying the torch for you."

It's going to be fun courting her again. Everyone says we belong together. In the last few weeks everyone we knew has called me to make sure I've seen Liza's picture in the *Times.* A guy at the health club shook his head with exasperation. "You let this bird fly away? You need your head examined. A wife like that is an asset."

That thought has, of course, occurred to me. I'm moving up the success ladder. But that's not the sole reason I want her back. I really do love her.

Liza

Myrna's eyes pop when Mark drops me off at the office. "He's *cute,"* she sighs. I have to admit I know how to pick ex-husbands. And married boyfriends. I knew Dan would be at Pierre's; it's his regular place. He looked fabulous. I looked fabulous. Mark looked fabulous. Isn't it nice how fabulous we all are? I just wanted to show him there are other fish in the sea, so who needs him? Big deal. What am I trying to prove? The man's married. Forget it. As they say in Russia, *tough shitsky.*

God knows what got into Mark, all that garbagio about getting together again. It's Rosalind, of course. I wish she'd butt out. She worries about me, I know. A husband is the most important thing. It doesn't matter to her how much money I make, how successful I am. When I asked her if she saw my picture in the *Times,* she said she'd rather it had been a wedding announcement.

> The mother fell on the mattress,
> And on the mattress she died.
> They didn't know what to call it
> So they called it matricide.

Mark certainly makes a nice appearance. *Cute,* as Myrna

says. I guess I can start going out with him and see what happens. Right now, I'm so thin-skinned, I can't trust my instincts about anyone. But so far as Mark's concerned, the wheel has turned. Who cares about Tiffany? She's no longer significant; the whole episode seems like a million years ago.

When I think about it, it wasn't the Tiffany thing that racked me out anyway. It was losing the baby. I wanted to die. I couldn't look at diaper commercials. There was a newborn in the building; one day, the baby was in the elevator when it got to my floor. I backed out, pretending I heard my phone.

I remember turning on Mark. "You're really relieved, aren't you? You really don't want to be a father, do you?"

Mark was genuinely shocked. How could I say such a thing?

I didn't know why I'd said it. The thought had just jumped into my mind. But as we stared at each other with tears in our eyes, we both knew it was the truth. Not that he had behaved badly. Tiffany was much later. He had stayed close to me, held me, wept with me, told me again and again that everything would be fine. But truth was truth. He had not wanted fatherhood then. Today at lunch, I didn't ask if he wanted fatherhood now.

"Don't think I'm giving up, Liza. I want you back, and I'm going to do everything I can to prove it," he said.

As a first step, he called a few minutes ago to say he's arranged a meeting with one of his investment clients, Multi-Regional Stores. It seems they'll be a prime sponsor of next year's Oscar Awards, and they're looking for new faces for their TV campaign, shopping mall fashion shows, and catalogs.

"That's really nice of you, Mark."

"Let's just say I'm good for something."

I am suddenly ravenous. Myrna is flabbergasted when I ask her to order me a cheese Danish and a hot chocolate.

"You just had lunch."

This happens to me all the time. When I'm strung out, I can't eat. The brook trout was delicious, but I couldn't swallow. I managed one radicchio leaf, which must have cost Mark twelve dollars. He didn't blink an eye.

You don't go to Pierre's to eat. You go to make deals and wage war. Come to think of it, when I passed Dan's table on our way out, I noticed his ears were red.

Maggie

I've got to get hold of myself. Why am I so frightened? Dan is back. I believe him when he says he's not seeing her. That crying jag the other night really scared me. It must have been the drinks. But there's not much chance of my turning into an alcoholic; I can't drink enough. Dan used to call me the cork-sniffer—one sniff and I was out like a light.

The doctor thinks hormone therapy might be a good idea. "But watch out. It can increase the libido!" he teases. "Dan's a lucky man." Wink, wink. I wish doctors would stop treating me like a birdbrain.

Sandi wouldn't talk to either of us for two whole days. This morning, she set the breakfast table to announce forgiveness and hugged me so hard I thought she'd never let go.

Dan just phoned. The Cunard Line is having a cocktail party, and he'd like me to join him. What's unsaid is that this is a test. Several years back, he stopped asking me to industry affairs for one simple reason: I kept making excuses to stay home, mainly because the kids might need me and I was afraid to leave them with a sitter. The fact is I was afraid all right, afraid of meeting the glamorous people in the travel business, terrified of their easy camaraderie and of not being able to make small talk. The worst was when strangers asked, "And what do you do?"

I'm only a housewife—it's impossible to say that with the conviction I feel about it. There was never a chance to expound on the importance of being a housewife, on its gratifications and its contribution to the health and development of our children. People smiled and turned away to find somebody more interesting. After a while, I couldn't take it anymore; and after a while, Dan stopped asking me to accompany him.

I know it bothered him. Sonia made it her business to tell me that. "Everyone asks where Dan's wife is, like he's ashamed of you. He always passes it off, but I can tell he's embarrassed. One woman asked me privately what was wrong—was Dan's wife a looney or an addict? Confidentially, someone had told her you weighed three hundred pounds and never left the house."

It's time to go public. Tonight I'll be the tall, slim, beautifully made-up, and expensively dressed wife. The mirror reassures me. I wear the same size I did when Dan and I got married. My bone structure is good. In trying to reassure me his affair was over, Dan said I was more beautiful than Liza, despite being ten years older. I was a classic beauty, he said. What's more, I looked younger than Liza.

Sandi and Jennifer say I look gorgeous and promise to be good. The doorman buzzes upstairs to say he's snagged me a cab. Stashed in my bag is a small medicine bottle filled with vodka, in case I need a jolt before I get to the hotel.

Liza

I'm on a roll. My scent is on the air. Good things are happening, and I'm scared to death something will go wrong. Irini is as sweet as she can be, which isn't all that sweet but is nonetheless bearable. Revlon is so ecstatic about Athena that they're thinking of creating a fragrance and cosmetics line around her. My idea is to call it *Zaziki,* after that yogurt and cucumber salad you find in the Greek islands. Smooth and creamy when you first taste it, it's loaded with garlic that suddenly hits you on the back of your tongue, an exciting combination of hot and cool. If the idea had come to me when I found Athena, I'd have named her *Zaziki,* a great name for a Greek model.

My Penrose family are turning out to be even better than I anticipated. I've booked the extra-tall girl for an extra-tall cake mix commercial, and I cut a deal for the boys with a rock group booker for a finder's fee up front and a percentage. Juliet Penrose is a Diana Ross clone with a fashion degree from the Rhode Island School of Design. She's put together an entirely new concept of interchangeable garments, fifty pieces that can combine to make 725 outfits, a kind of Rubik's Cube of endless possibilities. Two major chains have seen the line and are in the process of bidding.

Shakespeare said it: "Fame is the spur." The pursuit of a dream is an aphrodisiac, and achieving it is a satisfaction better than sex.

A month has gone by since the lunch at Pierre's. Dan is totally out of my system. I've totally stopped thinking about him. I'm cured. It was an aberration, a killer attack, like the tsetse fly. In retrospect, it's like I had a high fever. I was delirious. Now I've cooled down to normal. No scars. No aftereffects. It's as if it never happened.

Mark is becoming a problem. He thinks I'm kidding when I tell him that all I want is to be friends. He demands to know why I'm punishing him and why I won't sleep with him. We know from past experience how great we are in bed, don't we? Why am I so negative?

Lighten up, Mark. I'm not negative. I'm busy. If I'm married to my work, so be it. I can't wait to get up in the morning. I resent the hours I have to waste on sleep. Building a company is much more exciting than marriage. What I really need is a wife. In fact, I'm starting to hold auditions. What I'm looking for is a nice, amiable companion with an even disposition, good hygiene, and a boring personal history. No pets bigger than a goldfish. No police warrants. No ex-lovers of either sex wielding shotguns. Acceptable vices: chess, Scrabble, curry, all outdoor and indoor sports, and music of any kind at any volume, provided earphones are worn. Photography only with written permission.

My first job candidate is taking me to dinner Saturday. He doesn't know he's on a go-see. I won't tell him, of course; no point in getting him nervous. It's really a hoot. I feel like the Amazon queen in the old kids' comics, capturing male slaves for my personal, private pleasure. Not a bad idea.

Mark's on a new kick. He has decided to woo me, he says. He denies it's my mother's idea. "I came up with the idea myself. You're a romantic. I know how much you like being courted. That's what I've decided to do." All I can think is that he's reading one of those *How to Seduce Your Woman* books. Flowers, champagne, candy, and a hundred balloons tied with red ribbons have been arriving at intervals, like a Doris Day rerun. I have told him to cease and desist or I will have him arrested.

I can thank him for one thing: he has cured my chronic weakness for the romantic gesture. If I see one more coy greeting card or self-serving "ain't-I clever" surprise, I will rip his head off.

It was raining this morning, too wet to jog. I used the time to clear out my bedroom closet. How many skirts can one person wear! I separated the six or eight I do wear and bundled up the rest for the women's shelter. The last time I did this, I put a five-dollar bill in a pocket of each, thinking what a kick it would be for whoever wore it. Then I found out they dry-clean the clothes before distributing them.

In the back of the closet were three Food Emporium carrier bags of Dan's things—shirts, books, underwear. I wonder what he did with the red satin shorts, the bastard. There wasn't enough for the Salvation Army. I suppose I could have thrown it all in the trash. Then again, what's finished is finished. I figured I'd be a lady and have Myrna call his office to send a messenger to my office for the pickup.

Myrna has just told me Dan's secretary called back to say the messenger would come by at the end of the day. So that's that. File finally closed.

Daniel

All I wanted was to see her one more time. On neutral ground. By now we could be civil to each other, couldn't we? I told the receptionist to say the "messenger" had a personal message for her.

She nearly fell over when she saw me. "Hold all calls!" she told her secretary. She closed her office door.

"Do you want to make sure all your things are here?"

You really have to love a woman for that.

"I trust you, Liza."

"I trusted you, Daniel."

The stiletto, right between the ribs. I guess I deserved it. My car was downstairs. It was raining. It was rush hour. I insisted on dropping her home. She hesitated, as if she sensed the danger. The rain was pouring like Niagara Falls. She had no umbrella. There were no cabs.

Before we could stop it happening, we were right back where we started, alone together in our private world, hemmed in by rush-hour traffic and a curtain of rain.

The car radio played the blues. The traffic honked Gershwin in counterpoint. We didn't mean for it to happen, but we were helpless to stop it. It was so exciting to be making love inches away from other people and other cars.

Liza

We're back together. I should be ashamed, but I'm not. I can't help myself. I'm alive again. I'm happy. No, *ecstatic* is the word. Being alone with him in his car did it for both of us. The intimacy. The sweetness. The sheer excitement. I couldn't breathe. I thought if he didn't kiss me I would die. Great talk for a tough businesswoman, but that's how I felt, and that's how I feel.

We kissed. We hugged. We laughed. We found a Mars bar in the glove compartment and fed it to each other. We pretended it was all in fun, that that's as far as it would go, a friendly little flirtation till the gridlock eased. In a matter of seconds, it was like that first day in my apartment—no stopping, no thinking about consequences. We tore at each other in a gentle frenzy, finding the connecting passageways in the intricate maze of our clothes. Dan's back slammed against the steering wheel, the blaring horn adding a love tone to the symphony of dissonance outside.

We were cannibal beasts devouring each other. We were butterfly fingers on each other's flesh. We were oblivious to the storm and lucky it raged on. If the traffic had started to move, we would neither have seen nor heard.

As if coordinated by a force of nature, the storms inside and outside the car wore themselves out. The traffic inched its way free. We held hands but said nothing. We both knew what had happened.

"You still have it!" he said, back at my apartment. The

"engagement" ring he had bought me in California was on my dresser.

"I was going to throw it out the window."

"You'll hurt someone if you do that. Namely me."

He slipped it on the third finger of my left hand. "We can't fight it any longer. We belong together. Trust me, and give me a little time. A *very* little time, I promise. I'll work things out."

His marriage was all washed up. He and Maggie had both tried to make it work. He was unhappy. Maggie was unhappy, too, drinking and making scenes. A divorce could be the best thing that could happen to her. It would hurt, but it would force her to stand on her own two feet and take charge of her life. She was beautiful. She was good, a truly good woman. "She envies women like you, Liza."

"Me?" I was truly astounded. "She has everything!" Correction: *had* everything.

"It's my fault. She gave up her career for me."

"What was her career?"

"I thought I told you, she was a model. After we're married, maybe you can help her get started again."

"She'd love that, I'm sure."

His face as well as his ears reddened. "I can't believe I said that. I'm so happy, I can't think straight."

Passion spent, plans made, we said our goodbyes. It was getting late. His family had expected him home for dinner. He would wait until the girls were in bed and then tell Maggie he was leaving. He would move into a sublet, so that legally he would have a separate address, though actually he would be living with me—we'd be sleeping together every night, waking up together every morning.

My head is a whirling carousel. I'm going round and round, reaching for the gold ring. I can't let myself look too far into the future. I want this man. I want him now. The problems will have to solve themselves.

Maggie

I was kidding myself, living in a fool's paradise. I thought we'd patched things up. He was making love to me again. He told me how proud of me he was at the Cunard party, everyone rushing over to meet me and say how much they'd heard about me and that I was even prettier and nicer than Dan said. Several people asked me what I did. This time I had prepared myself.

"I've been a homemaker while the children were small. Now they're both in school, so I'm looking for a job. Any ideas?"

It was a speech I had rehearsed innumerable times in my mind. Now it flowed easily from my lips. Two men gave me their cards and told me to call them. It was frightening but exciting.

"See, darling? If you really want to go back to work, they're waiting with open arms."

It was all so wonderful. I threw away the medicine bottle of vodka. No more crutches for me. I was so happy. I can just picture myself grinning from ear to ear like a jackass. It was all too good to be true, and that's how it's turned out.

The minute Dan walked through the door, I knew something was wrong. It had been raining all day, and when the storm blew up at about six o'clock, I could feel it in my bones—a sense of foreboding, an accident maybe. I knew he had the car and was probably stuck in traffic, unable to call to say he'd be late. I kept looking out the window, even though I wouldn't have been able to see him in the rain. Ambulances and police cars were racing through the park, sirens shrieking. There are always more accidents in the rain. What if this time it was Dan? When I saw his face, I knew something worse had happened.

"I take full responsibility," he said. Sure, that's what they all say. Terrorists, hijackers, men who dump toxic waste, politicians, drug companies. Kill a few people, wreck a few lives. What the hell does that *mean*, full responsibility? Does that absolve him? Is that it? He takes full responsibility?

He thinks it best if he goes to a hotel tonight.

"You mean to her!"

"I said a hotel, Maggie. It will give us both some breathing room." He'll come by in the morning for coffee if it's okay with me. Okay with me? It's not okay. How could it be okay? My husband is leaving me!

I had so much to tell him tonight. This morning I had my interview with Ed Phillips, the guy I met at the Cunard party. He publishes a magazine for travel agents and is looking for someone to sell advertising space. No salary, of course, but a nice, healthy commission. He thinks I'd be perfect. I had wanted to discuss it with my husband, but I no longer have a husband.

What's happening to the world? I don't understand. Is it such a crime to have a happy marriage? Or unfashionable? Does it make the gods jealous? Do they turn green with envy when they see a happy family? Do they say, "Those people are too happy. Let's have some fun and break it up"?

Maybe the gods are gay!

Daniel

I know Maggie thinks I'm at Liza's. I called her after I checked into the hotel to say where I was.

"I don't care where you are."

"I meant in case you need me."

"I need you to be my husband."

"I'll see you in the morning, Maggie. We can talk then."

I need this time alone to think. I call Liza to say good night and tell her where I am and that I love her and will call her tomorrow.

She asks if I want to come over. I ache to be with her, but I feel almost religious about this decision. I need to be by myself in impersonal surroundings while I try to figure out the next step.

Maggie

Knowing you're about to hear bad news doesn't make it any easier. Dignity and pride become a major consideration. It's like going to the guillotine. Screaming, begging, and crawling won't save you, so the best course is to hold your head high and accept your fate with grace.

I've never been good at making scenes. I've secretly envied the women who rant and shriek and smash furniture and throw drinks in restaurants. There's one betrayed wife who took scissors and cut out the crotch of all her husband's trousers.

Everyone says how awful, but these women get what they want. They don't care what people think. The man with the butchered suits came back to his wife; he hadn't realized how passionately she loved him.

I can't do that sort of thing, it's against my nature. I was brought up to be civilized, to deal with situations with restraint. I am admired for my self-control, my talent for moderating family conflicts. I am an absolute saint, a perfect lady—and what has it gotten me?

My husband has left me for another woman. I slept alone last night on his side of the bed. Every time I closed my eyes I could see him with her, touching her and kissing her and holding her and saying things to her he hasn't said to me in years. I never realized I was capable of such erotic imaginings, such vivid, close-up mental details of their sexual rituals and pleasures. I felt that I was in bed with them, invisible and totally ignored. Yet I could not stop watching them in my imagination—their lips, their hands, their writhing naked bodies, their eyes closed in ecstasy, my husband's mounting cries of *Liza, Liza, Liza, Liza, LIZA*—

Now it's morning. I have dark circles under my eyes. Let him see what he's done to me, if he can see straight at all. He's come for coffee and to talk. I like the idea of putting arsenic in his coffee, but I'm fresh out of arsenic. Instead, and despite my anger, I've made his favorite breakfast, French toast. He thanks me politely, but he's not hungry.

"Just coffee."

The bastard, he knows what trouble it is to make French toast. I want to say something sarcastic, like how come he skipped jogging this morning. Instead, I accidentally knock over a full container of fresh-squeezed orange juice. He tries to help me mop it up. I push him away with a violence that startles us both.

"You don't live here anymore, Dan!"

The girls have heard the commotion. I had told them to stay in their rooms and get ready for school, that Daddy and I had some private things to talk about. Dan is relieved to see them. He looks particularly well this morning—tall, handsome Daddy.

"My two glamor girls!"

They can't help themselves. They shout with delight and hurl themselves at him. "Daddy, Daddy—you're back!"

I could quite calmly drive a steak knife through his heart. And twist it to make sure. He puts his arms around my daughters and gathers them to his manly chest. He can't see the happiness and relief on their faces, but I can.

"I love you both so much and I miss you so much I can hardly stand it—"

Both girls sense the impending *but.* They break away from him, their eyes imploring him for a miracle, their bodies braced for the terrible *but.*

"But something has happened, something you won't understand until you're all grown up. Mommy and I are getting a divorce. I'm still your father. I still love you very much—"

Jennifer shrieks and collapses on his neck. "Please, Daddy, no! I'll be good, I promise, I'll get straight A's. I'll clean my room. I'll take care of Sandi. I'll help Mom. I'll do anything you say. I promise, please—"

Sandi clings to his thigh, adding her cries to the cacophony of grief. "Don't go, Daddy. Don't go. I'll never wet the bed again. It was an accident. Daddy, please—"

"Maggie—please!" He's panicking. Now *he's* saying *please.*

"Please what?" What does he expect me to do?

"Please, Maggie—I didn't want it to be like this."

"How did you want it to be? Your wife and children throwing rose petals in your path and giving you going-away gifts?"

He disengages his frantic children and makes for the door. Sandi turns her fury on me, her small fists hammering at me as hard as she can. Jennifer runs sobbing from the room.

"I'm sorry, Maggie."

"You should be sorry." He should be dead.

"You don't have to be like that."

"How should I be?" Little Mary Sunshine?

"Look, I've got an important meeting."

His talk of an important meeting was always the signal for me to express my wifely support, to tell him how brilliant he is, how well he's going to handle things. From habit, I nearly fall into the old routine, and from habit, despite our changed circumstance, he seems to be expecting the old "you're-wonderful, you-can-do-anything" routine, too.

Instead, I say I hope the meeting proves lucrative, because he's going to need a lot of money.

"I'll speak to you later, Maggie."

"Don't call me. Call my lawyer."

"Lawyer? What lawyer? Can't we just talk?"

"Daniel, you have left me."

"I know I've left you."

"You are living with another woman."

"I know I'm living with another woman."

"You have asked me for a divorce, and don't tell me you know you've asked for a divorce. I know you've asked for a divorce. Our children know you've asked for a divorce. There's nothing more to be said. You've said it all. Talk to my lawyer. I can't stand the sight of you."

When the door slams between us, I look at my husband through the peephole as he waits for the elevator. Old habits are hard to break. It still gives me a voyeuristic thrill. I will have to get over it.

There's no two ways about it, leaving home has changed his appearance, taken years off his life. I was wrong about the jogging. It wasn't dangerous for his health, it was dangerous for my health. He's slimmed down and he's tan, looking just like he did that first morning in this apartment fifteen years ago, when I stood at the peephole for one last glance at my handsome new husband as he left for work.

I thanked God every day for Dan and the miracle of our marriage. It was at the height of the sexual revolution. Women were free to experiment with sex and take as many lovers as they liked. I wasn't against the new freedom. I was simply too shy and too inhibited. I envied other women. I had my share of open relationships, but I was a washout. I tried but I couldn't get it on, or take it off for that matter, not with someone I'd just met. One man called me the Icicle and broke a popper under my nose. Another took me back to his loft and with no preliminaries said, "Down on your knees," and gave me explicit guidance on how to proceed.

Dan was just starting out in the travel business. Our courtship was very old-fashioned. I was a showroom model at a better sportswear house on Seventh Avenue, hoping to use my fashion training to become a designer, although I was too shy to push myself. Dan and I met at a crowded cocktail party. I was standing alone in a corner, pretending to read a magazine. He took me to dinner, and weeks later he said I reminded him of Joan Fontaine in *Rebecca.*

The night he got me to unclip my barrette and loosen my hair and open the top three buttons of my blouse, he proposed;

and when he finished undressing me, I surprised both of us with the reckless abandon of my passion.

"You are everything to me," he said. "You're the perfect combination—the straitlaced wife in public, the mistress of my wildest fantasies in bed. I will love you forever and ever."

The public wife continued to be straitlaced. Often he would ask me to wear my hair loose, and I did it to please him, but I felt uncomfortable. With my hair scraped back and the barrette holding it tightly in place, I felt safe. After the children arrived, the wild fantasies became a private joke. Occasionally, we made a self-conscious ritual of celebrating a birthday or anniversary, but gradually we agreed we were an old married couple and deeply content with our affectionate and loving sex life.

I knew something was going wrong the night he pushed my hand away and said he needed his sleep because he had decided to start jogging. The travel business was a young man's game. He was getting flabby. A corporate client had called him "sir" and treated him like Methuselah. He was determined to get back in shape, for my sake as well as his. I didn't want to lose him, did I? After a certain age a man had to exercise—or atrophy.

I was supportive about his jogging, but for the wrong reasons. I had been afraid I would lose him to a heart attack. I was so goddam smug and secure in my marriage, I was too stupid to sense the real danger. And now I have lost everything—my husband, my marriage, the support system I so carefully created for our children.

"Mom-my!" Jennifer is in the bathroom, calling me. "Mommy! Hurry!" Her voice spirals upward in a fearsome shriek. "I'm *bleeding!*"

Has she cut her wrists in a melodramatic act of life imitating art, according to the gospel of TV—only to find a razor can hurt? "Jennifer! Open the door this instant."

What I find is proof of nature's ability to flourish in the darkest of circumstances. A young girl's first menstruation should be a milestone for rejoicing in the bosom of her family. Not this time. Welcome to womanhood, my daughter.

Daniel

Maggie said it was okay to come by and pick up some more of my things. She's surprisingly composed, and she greets me as if I'm an encyclopedia salesman she's sorry she agreed to see and whose spiel she must now endure. She looks different. Instead of her usual slacks and shirt, she's wearing the brown suit she had on the night of the Cunard party. She handled herself beautifully that night. Everyone asked where had she been hiding. She finally relaxed and enjoyed herself, or said she did. One thing I know: her hands were like ice, a sure sign of panic. But she didn't let it show.

"You look very nice today, Maggie."

"So you told me at the Cunard bash."

"I meant it then, and I mean it now. A lot of people called to say what a beautiful, stylish woman you are." A little square compared to the Other Woman, Sonia said. Sonia makes a second career of finding fault. Too old-fashioned-looking, a throwback to the fifties, Sonia said. I reminded Sonia that she was the only woman alive who remembered the fifties, that Maggie was in grammar school, so quit picking on her.

"Won't they be confused when you tell them you're running out on your beautiful, stylish wife? What will they think when they meet Liza? How does she rank in the beautiful and stylish ratings? Sonia told me to give the brown suit to the senior citizens' shelter. She says it makes me look like my grandmother. Perhaps that's where I went wrong. You don't like being seen out with your grandmother."

"Sonia's getting senile. How could you listen to her? I love you in this suit—"

"Love me?"

"Wasn't I with you when we bought it?"

"Maybe you want me to be dowdy and old. Helen was telling me about a neighbor of theirs in Phoenix, Janice—Janice lived her whole life in the sun, and her face was starting to look like an alligator. She wanted to have one of those skin peels, you know, that leaves your face soft and pink as a baby's behind. Her husband said no dice, he loved her the way she was. A month later, he ran away with all their money and a twenty-year-old bank teller."

"I am not running away, Maggie. I am going to do the best I can for you and the children. I guarantee your life-style, their education, everything the same as it is now."

"Except for one thing."

"Yes, Maggie, except for one thing. I plan to marry Liza as soon as possible."

"And what about your second family, the children you'll have with her? Where does that leave Jennifer and Sandi, may I ask that? Do they get cut out of your will?"

I haven't thought about my will. "You are obsessed with death, Maggie. Heart attacks, wills. I'm a young man. The girls are my heirs. If and when Liza and I have a child, I'll do what needs to be done then—and not before."

"I don't believe you've thought this thing out, Dan. All the permutations and consequences."

I have to admit I haven't. "The point is, I want everything to be on the up and up, no sneaking around, no more lies and deception. I'm being honest with you, Maggie. I'm in love with Liza. She's in love with me. We want to be married. The details are something you and I will have to work out."

"What makes you think I'm willing to work things out?"

That stops me in my tracks. "Well—why wouldn't you want to work things out? Why would you want to stay married to someone who wants to marry someone else? How nice can that be for you?"

"Not very nice at all, I assure you. But let's look at it from my point of view. The way I see it, you're going through another stage of mid-life crisis."

"Maggie, for God's sake. Not that again."

"The way I see it, this is a difficult time for both of us. So what I've decided to do is give you my blessings."

"Oh, Maggie, I've always said what a special person you are—"

"It's not what you think. I'm not saying go ahead, have your divorce. I'm saying you have my blessings—and my permission—to let the affair run its course. You vowed to be my husband for better or for worse. We have a joint investment in this marriage and in our children. You might as well know now I will never agree to a divorce. You can get one without my consent, but I'll drag you through the courts for the next fifty years!"

Would I like some coffee? I have come for morning coffee, haven't I? She made a fresh pot.

"Half-and-half?"

"No, thanks."

"When did you stop having cream with your coffee?"

"It causes phlegm."

"Oh, really? Is that what Liza says?"

"Leave Liza out of this—"

"Oh, Dan. Come *on*—"

It was admittedly a dumb thing to say.

"I'm sorry, Maggie. I was hoping this could be an amicable divorce."

"I'm sorry, too." She looks up at the kitchen clock. "We'll have to continue our talk another time. I have an important appointment downtown."

My hackles rise. "With a lawyer?"

"If you must know, it's a job interview. But remember, Dan, you moved out. You don't live here anymore. You no longer have the right to ask where I'm going or who I'm seeing."

She declines my offer to share a cab downtown.

"One more thing—" Have I broken the news to Sonia?

Sonia

I really don't need this aggravation. Dan doesn't seem to realize I'm in this, too. He and I are partners. If Maggie gets a smart divorce lawyer like Raoul Felder, they can tie up our assets for months. Years. In court. Out of court. Depositions. Hearings. That's all we need, a court order to examine the books. I'm too old for this. I'm getting ready to buy a condominium in Boca and retire. I do not need any court-appointed accountants going through our books. The next thing you know, the IRS will be sending in the storm troops, and we'll all be in *schtuck.*

"What's your hurry? Why not live with her for a while, see how you like it?"

"I love her and I want to marry her."

"I understand what you're saying."

"No you don't, Sonia. You're refusing to understand what I'm saying. You think this is just some little cheapo affair and it'll go away. Maggie thinks so, too. Well, it's not a cheap affair. We love each other and we are determined to get married. Don't worry about the money. I'll take care of everything. Maggie and the children will get their fair share."

"Don't underestimate Maggie. Do you have any gold fillings?"

"Why, yes—do they show?"

"Maggie's going to get those and everything else. Mark my words. It's the quiet ones who turn nasty."

There's no point trying to reason with him. He's in *love.* My God, he's forty-five years old; the next thing you know he'll have *babies,* and then what? He says he wants me to meet Liza. He knows I will love her as much as he does.

The man needs help, but he's given me an idea. I'm going to call Liza and invite her to lunch, just the two of us.

Maggie

I lied to Dan. I didn't have a job interview. I had nothing whatsoever to do. Not a goddam thing. I waited until Dan's cab disappeared and walked around aimlessly for a couple of hours. The pleasantness of the day lured me into Central Park, and soon I found myself drawn inexorably to the reservoir. The early morning joggers were long gone. A few daytime people maintained a hypnotic pace. This was the scene of the original crime. I wondered where an invisible X marked the spot where they first met. I should have gone running with him. I should never have let him out by himself.

"Bad move!" my old friend Nina said. "Big mistake." I hadn't seen or spoken to Nina in months, until I called her last night after Dan left. She and Ralph and Dan and I had been a regular foursome until Ralph left her and they divorced. It's hard for a married woman and a divorcée to maintain an ongoing friendship. She didn't like being a threesome at dinner. I honestly didn't know any eligible men to introduce to her. Dan was particularly uncooperative. "I don't know any men. Anyway, she's too picky. I've heard her. Nobody's good enough. Let her find her own chump."

Ralph had actually left her for a man. Otherwise, my situation was the same—dumped with two children. She did what I know I should do: get a good lawyer, then a good settlement, followed by a good wardrobe, a good job, and last but not least, a good lover, preferably young.

Despite her exciting, glamorous, and fun-filled life, Nina was free to have dinner tonight and promised to give me the lowdown on exactly what to do.

Meantime, I found myself on the east side of the Park with a choice of going to the Metropolitan Museum of Art or the Guggenheim. I had looked up Liza's address in the phone book. Her apartment was close by. It was such a nice day, I decided to walk by her building and see what it was like.

Liza

My mother has totally wigged out. She went so far as to say, "What have I done to deserve this?" It continues to amaze me how the whole world revolves around her. When I married Mark, the relatives and friends congratulated *her.* When we divorced, they gathered at her house as if somebody had died.

"I'm not dead, Rosalind. I'm divorced. Hundreds of people get divorced every day. Men and women. And after a while, they marry someone else."

"Men get divorced and marry someone else. Women sit home and wait for the phone to ring."

That was not going to happen to me. I did not leave a husband for Dan. Dan left his wife for me. Would she at least do me a favor and meet him? She was more upset than I ever would have expected.

She didn't want to meet him.

And if I persisted in this stupidity, she didn't want to speak to me because she was afraid she'd say things she'd regret. "For the time being, I'm so upset, it's better to say nothing."

To compound things, Dan is being a genuine pain in the ass. It's not that I don't love him and want to marry him, but he's exposing a side of his character I haven't seen before. He's all sulky and pouty when he can't have what he wants.

He hates the hotel where he's staying; but like I keep telling him, it's only temporary, until he finds a sublet, which should be any second. He wants to move in with me. We both know he can't. He's got to get his lawyer to file for a separation, and even then, he's still not safe. Technically, he can't cohabit with me.

He's got to have his own separate legal address, and that's all there is to it.

Maggie may hire detectives. It all seems so silly. Everyone knows we're sleeping together. But it's not so silly where children are concerned. If he wants to see his children, he's got to have a place of his own where they can visit him. He can't bring them to my place. Think what a judge would say to that. Poor kids, they wouldn't like it either. The thought of his children makes me sad. It's going to take time, I know. They may never like me. I'll just have to be patient and caring and hope they'll accept me eventually.

Dan thinks all my caution is ridiculous. This afternoon he got real crabby. He announced that he planned to stay over with me tonight. No way, I said. "You can stay until four in the morning, but that's it. You can't be seen leaving with me or going to work as if you lived with me."

I haven't told him his beloved partner called to invite me to lunch. I'm curious to hear what she has to say.

Mark has also asked me to lunch. Rosalind has given up on the Perfect Remarriage. She did, however, fill him in on my new status as homewrecker. One thing about scandal: people insist on buying you a meal.

Maggie

Approaching Liza's building, my heart began to pound. I felt like a burglar casing the joint, like any minute somebody would grab me by the arm and say, "What are you doing here?" It's a free country. I have every right to walk down the street.

Her building is large and undistinguished, like so much of

the East Side residential construction of the sixties; it has none of the charm of the West Side. But it's expensive as hell, I'm sure. Nina moved to the East Side after her divorce. She pays three thousand dollars a month for an apartment half the size of ours.

Liza must be very successful to afford this. She's the smart one, not me. I gave up my career, and now look at me. She doesn't depend on a man for support. She makes her own money and then looks around and picks out a man like she picks out a new fur coat: "I'll take that one. That one will keep me warm on winter nights."

Her doorman looks like a general in the Albanian Army; he has a much fancier uniform than ours. As I strolled by, he left his post to carry some luggage down the street to a waiting car. It was an invitation. I walked past the All Visitors Must Be Announced sign and through the lobby—thick rugs, richly covered furniture, paintings, mirrors, chandeliers, and real trees in giant pots (no plastic here). My husband was moving up in the world. In the mail room, I looked at the list and found her name and her apartment number, 10-D. *D* for Daniel. How adorable.

I was about to leave when the elevator door opened. Another invitation. Riding up to the tenth floor, I suddenly had to bend over to keep from fainting. The door of 10-D looked like every other door; there was nothing to distinguish it as a love nest. Damn her, I was going to scratch her eyes out. It felt good to think this as I rang her bell. She would not be there, of course. She was downtown, running her modeling empire. The door opened. A young black man in jeans and a T-shirt stood there. "Yeah?"

What did she have, a male harem? Or was it a *ménage à trois?* Was this what seduced Dan—threesies orgies? No wonder I couldn't compete with that. The man turned out to be from the housecleaning service that does Liza's apartment once a week. He gave me his card. I peered past him into the apartment. All I could make out were splashes of bright colors mixed with white and lots of windows. Since I had attributed my intrusion to being on the wrong floor, I couldn't think of an excuse to go in.

I was frightened and excited by my temerity. Who'd have thought shy, retiring Maggie would have had the nerve to pull a stunt like this? Crossing the lobby, I could see the doorman had returned to his post. "Good morning," I said warmly, wondering if he would challenge my presence in the building. I could easily have slit someone's throat and had their diamonds and securities in my shoulder bag.

He saluted me with a nod and a smile. With a building this size, he didn't know everyone personally. It occurred to me it would be easy to return without being announced.

Daniel

Liza can't have dinner with me tonight. She's got a business meeting in Connecticut at five and doesn't expect to get back until late.

"So what am I supposed to do?"

"What do you mean?" She sounds perplexed and impatient, a tone of voice that really pisses me off.

"I mean that I am living in a hotel room. By myself. None of my belongings. What am I supposed to do? Have dinner in the coffee shop and watch TV?"

"Daniel, I'm sorry. I'm a businesswoman. I'm not the 'little woman.' If you want pipe and slippers, go back to Maggie!"

Ten seconds later, she calls back to apologize. "I'm sorry I said that, darling. I know you've moved out of your comfortable home. We'll talk about it when I get back. Maybe we can have a little late supper together, okay?"

A little while later, an envelope arrives. It contains the sublet listings from the *Times*, *New York* magazine, and *7 Days*. Several Upper East Side apartments are circled in red and punctuated with little hearts along with the notation "Walking distance from L's apartment."

Sublets; all she talks about is sublets. Has she seen any of these places? Purple walls. Tiger-skin bedspreads. Leaky radiators. Windows on air shafts, if there are windows. And the rents are out of sight—three or four thousand a month for two bedrooms. And I need two bedrooms. When my girls come to visit me, there's no way I'm going to put them on the living room couch.

"It's only temporary," Liza insists. "That's what a sublet is for, a temporary place to live. Once we're married, we'll find a bigger place together—with a separate bedroom for the girls."

When I look more closely at the listings, I recognize several as ones I have seen. One new one sounds promising. The woman on the phone is asking five thousand a month, plus a ten-thousand-dollar deposit against damage and loss.

Who does Liza think I am, Donald Trump? Ten thousand dollars deposit? Nobody ever gives back a deposit. They always find something, like a scratch on the Chippendale desk. I've got to make her understand I'm not made of money. I'll have an ex-wife to support and two little girls to send through college.

What does Liza know about children? Maggie's no spendthrift, but last winter when we were invited to that wedding at the Regency, she bought the girls party dresses at a hundred dollars a clip. Bicycles, CDs, braces, it's out of sight. Jennifer thinks nothing of asking me for twenty dollars so she can meet her girlfriends for lunch at the Hard Rock Cafe.

There's no way I'm going to pay thousands of dollars a month rent on some roach-infested sublet. Liza and I are going to have to talk.

Liza

Why can't he get the lead out? It's not all that complicated to rent a sublet. Why does he complicate things? The divorce was his idea, wasn't it? Suddenly, it's like I pushed him into it, like it's my fault he's living in a hotel, or my fault he's lonely at night.

"Liza, what am I supposed to do?"

I had to bite my tongue. I wanted to say, "Play with yourself, dammit, and get off my case!" Here I am on my way to Connecticut, in stage four of a major negotiation for a multimillion-dollar budget involving location shooting in five countries and print, television, and video cassettes for in-store promotions.

I've been working on my figures for days in order to come up with the most sensible budget for them and the biggest profits for me. The physical office work alone can give you shingles. Over forty people will be at this meeting. I hired two computer artists to jazz up the proposal, had the whole thing color-copied on subject-coded stock and bound in red vinyl folders, and ordered matching red vinyl notepads and shiny red pens engraved "Liza Central" for everyone attending.

I had Myrna hire a calligrapher to help assemble the envelopes and handwrite each recipient's name in ink. Driving up to Connecticut, I am in no mood for Daniel's problems. It's a drag, man! As I'm telling him about a seven-figure deal, he's telling me he's lonely in his hotel room. *Poor little baby.* What did he think I was going to do, cancel my meeting and go running over there with chicken soup?

Wait till he hears I'm going to England next week. I've just changed the name of one of my new models to Chelsea Britt. She's the daughter of a British diplomat; she was raised here and in England. I think she's ready for a major launch, and I've arranged several meetings in London—and maybe I'll jump over to Paris for a few days.

This little separation will give him plenty of time to get cracking with his lawyer and find a sublet. I love the man. I want to marry him. I want to live happily ever after—but not ten years down the road.

I want it now.

Maggie

I'm feeling better tonight, more in control. I'm giving a few orders instead of taking them, and I'm making plans of my own without consulting anyone. This divorce thing may be just what I need.

I'm meeting Nina at eight. The sitter called to cancel, but did I panic? Did I call Nina to cancel? Hell, no. I called my soon-to-be-ex husband and told—not asked, *told*—him he could take the girls to dinner and stay with them until I got back. I didn't ask about his plans for the evening; I really didn't care what he and Liza were doing. If he wanted to see Sandi and Jennifer, here was his chance. And he jumped at it.

"Maggie—" His voice sounded odd. "Thanks."

Jennifer insisted on doing my eye makeup.

"I'm only meeting another woman."

"You never know, Mom. The Pizza Mia is a pickup palace for the over-thirty set."

"Where did you hear that?" Nina had picked the place.

"That's what it said in *7 Days.*"

A pickup palace for the over-thirties. That's us. Nina says she goes there all the time. It sounds like as good a place as any to start my new life as a single. Before meeting Nina, I drop by the school gym. Once a month, the neighborhood volunteers get together to exchange war stories about garbage, doggie doo, rats, illegal renovations, street crime, ghetto blasters, prostitutes, pushers—the usual.

"Maggie, what happened to you?"

"You look fabulous!"

"Hey, gang, get a load of Maggie."

I have not made any public announcements about the divorce. I realize none of them have ever really seen me in anything but pants and a shirt. Tonight I'm dolled up in a short skirt and an old velvet jacket I forgot I had, with a red satin blouse Sonia gave me three years ago, which I've never worn.

"Why have you been hiding those legs?"

Freddy and I have been old campaigners for years, organizing rallies, going down to City Hall, handing out petitions. All of a sudden he's looking at me strangely. My God, the man is flirting with me!

"I'll bet you say that to all the girls," is about the best I can do in the circumstances. I'm new at this.

"So-o-o-o-o-" He's devouring me with his eyes.

"So-o-o-o-o-"

"So how's Dan?"

The gang is watching. This seems as good a time as any. "Oh—haven't you heard? We've split."

Freddy is the professional Extra Man, divorced for many years. In fact, there's a rumor that he's never been married. Several female—and a few male—volunteers have made plays for him, without success.

"Is it true? Are you really getting a divorce?"

"Dan's moved out."

Freddy tells me how sorry he is, that if I need a strong shoulder to cry on, I can call on him anytime; and as a matter of fact, why don't we have dinner so I can tell him all about it? He pats my hand. "I'm a very good listener."

"Call me!"

"What about tonight?"

"Sorry—I have a date."

Nina has already established herself at the far end of the Pizza Mia bar. "Maggie! Come over and meet the two best-looking dudes in New York."

The two men on either side of her stand and make a place for me beside her. They are also regulars at Pizza Mia, Victor and Terry. Both are conservatively dressed and in their fifties or maybe sixties—these days it's hard to tell. Nina looks spectacular—her hair, makeup, and clothes look like something out of a magazine. I feel dowdy in comparison.

Victor asks, "You live alone?"

"She's in the process of divorce," Nina explains. She whispers in my ear. "If we play it right, they'll buy us dinner."

"I thought we were going to talk," I whisper back.

Terry has ordered champagne all around. Nina dips her finger in her glass and flicks it behind Terry's earlobe. "It means good luck."

"Another time, Nina love. I've got to get on my horse."

As if on cue, the maitre d' tells Nina her table is ready.

Victor says, "Enjoy your dinner, girls."

"He really likes you, Maggie," Nina assures me when we are seated. "I can tell from the way he looked at you."

"He's not looking at me now!" It's all foolishness. Nina is just trying to make me feel good. The restaurant is jammed with wonderful-looking people. If it's the over-thirty set, they don't look it, especially the women. They all look as if they're on college vacation—a European college, to hear the clatter of French, Italian, and German surrounding us.

"Well—" she says, after we've ordered.

"Well, Nina, it's good to see you."

She raises her glass. "Welcome to the club."

"The club?"

"The Manhattan AC—the Alimony Club."

"Well—this is all a new situation for me. We haven't really discussed things yet."

She leans toward me. "Two rules, Maggie. Two rules if you want to survive. Get a piranha for a lawyer. And take everything he's got."

"I won't have to do that with Dan. He'll do the right thing. I want to be fair."

"Never, *never* say that word again. Listen to what I say."

This is my introduction to the world of divorced women. I listen carefully, considering myself lucky to have an old friend like Nina to tell me the score. When Ralph walked out, she nearly fell apart. Their son ran away to the East Village, which saved her from a nervous breakdown because she had someone else to think of besides herself. She walked the streets until she found him, put him in therapy for two years, and now he's fine, a freshman at UCLA, "as far away from his parents as he can go."

Ralph was so smitten with his new boyfriend that he was willing to agree to anything. "An-y-thing! So I took ev-er-y-thing! And every month, when that alimony check arrives, I open a bottle of Moët & Chandon and drink a toast to myself. The cocksucking bastard. Living well *is* the best revenge, especially when it's on your ex-husband's money!"

She knocks back her glass of red wine and snaps furiously for the waiter to bring another. Behind the laminated facade, she is trembling.

"And you know what else?"

The pizza, so rich and delicious moments before, is like chalk in my mouth. I can barely speak. "What else?"

"If his check is one day late, I take him to court. I still have charge cards in his name. He's sent letters to the stores, but I always find some salesgirl who doesn't know any better. I charge and take, he gets the bill. See these bangles? From my latest raid. Wait till he gets the bill. Nice, eh?"

I take a good look at her wrist. It is so thin, the bone sticks out like a knob. Her hands look old, the veins popping up blue through the taut skin, the nails long and simonized. When I first walked into Pizza Mia, she had looked so young and vivacious at the bar. Now it might be the lighting or the wine, or because I am really looking at her, but she looks old and haggard, her throat all crepey, with a bracket of deep lines from nose to chin and lip gloss splaying out from her mouth in rivulets of red.

I try changing the subject. "What are you doing?"

"What do you think I'm doing? Surviving, that's what I'm doing. Living from day to day, trying to find a new man like one of those turds at the bar, that's what I'm doing."

She is drunk. I am feeling a slight buzz. Seeing her like this brings me down with a crash. More than anything, I want to leave. I want to get up and leave her and run out into the street, anywhere to get away from her. This is not what it was going to be like. I don't want to be like Nina. I won't be a member of her Alimony Club.

"I meant work. Didn't you open a shop? Art Deco or something?"

"I sold it. Doubled my investment. Lucky in money. Unlucky in love. What are your plans? A needlepoint boutique? Catering service? Interior decorator? Where would we be without divorced women!"

I had looked forward to seeing Nina. I had made a mental list of all the questions I wanted to ask, all the fears and hopes I wanted to discuss. She'd been through the wars and looked and seemed so together, I had thought she could advise me, give me a few tips for my new life.

For a few hours today I had almost convinced myself Dan was doing me a favor and that divorce was the best thing that could happen to me. The spurious sense of freedom and power, the compliments on my legs, Freddy trying to date me, this Victor at the bar asking me if I live alone. Pathetic crumbs. If that's what divorced women live on, I'll die of starvation.

Victor has remained at the bar throughout our dinner. He is watching us when the coffee arrives. The waiter indicates him when we ask for the check.

Nina beams with pleasure. "Victor's picked up the tab." She sends him a kiss.

I pretend to be dazzled by the gesture. "You see, Nina. It's you he really wants. The man looks smitten to me."

Her face registers naked contempt. "Don't be a twat, Maggie. Grow up. He'd take either of us. You don't live alone. I do. This is the real world, so you'd better get used to it. You know something else? I've always envied you. I thought you must know something, or have some little secret between your legs. Mrs. Happily Married, the Perfect Wife with your perfect home and perfect children and perfect husband. Well, like I said, welcome to the club. This is all you can expect. And don't look so mother superior at me, dearie. I've got a warm body to sleep with tonight. You'll be sleeping alone."

When she closes in on me for the ritual air kiss, a shiver goes through me. She's not laminated; she's embalmed.

The street outside confuses me. I'm not sure where I am. I can't just stand there waiting for a cab. I've got to move, to get away. I start to run for block after block, until I'm out of breath. The street sign tells me I'm around the corner from Liza's. Dan is with the children. She'll be alone in that fancy apartment of hers. Waiting for him. You've got a long wait, sister. He can't leave the children until I get home.

I inhale deeply to calm myself. The fresh air has cleared my brain of the wine. I check out my appearance in a storefront to be sure I won't look like a lunatic when I approach the doorman.

There's nobody on duty. I walk in and take the elevator to the tenth floor. No sounds come from Liza's apartment. I ring tentatively at first and then louder and louder. Where the hell are you, dammit? I need to speak to you!

"Answer the door, damn you!" I can hear my voice rising. I am banging on the door, kicking it as hard as I can. "Open the door this minute, you bitch. I've got something to say to you!"

My passion exhausted, I collapse against the door, my chest heaving in pain. Thank God she isn't home. I must be crazy. I am blowing my nose and getting ready to leave when I hear the elevator stop. *Liza.* Who else can it be? She can't find me here. I'll die. My God, how could I do such a thing? As the elevator door opens, I see the fire exit across the hall from 10-D and make a mad dash through the door.

I am standing there, panting. My legs are like jelly. I can hear keys and a door opening and slamming shut. I'm afraid to move or to make a noise. Should I creep down the stairs? What if I'm locked in the stairwell? What if a burglar alarm goes off? Or maybe it's a silent alarm, and the police are already on the way. My arms are paralyzed. My only escape is the way I got in. I am desperately trying to open the door to the corridor when it flies open. Liza is threatening me with a tennis racket.

"Don't move or I'll beat your fucking brains out! Who the hell are you?"

"I'm—I'm Maggie—"

"Maggie who? What do you want?"

"I'm Dan's wife."

"My God—"

"I want you to give me back my husband."

Daniel

I knew I missed them, but I didn't realize how much. They were a little standoffish at first, Jennifer in particular. But soon it was like I'd never left. We flipped a coin to see where we'd eat. Jennifer wanted hamburgers, Sandi wanted southern-fried chicken. Jennifer won the call, two out of three. Sandi said it wasn't fair. I remembered a place on Columbus Avenue that serves both.

I bought presents for each of them, and we walked home eating tofutti cones. Sandi tripped and dropped hers. I gave her mine. By the time Maggie got home, the three of us were cuddled together, watching tapes.

Maggie had left the house before I arrived to pick the girls up. I had not seen her in this particular outfit. I gave out a low wolf whistle. Both girls giggled. "What a pair of gams. I hope you two inherit your mom's legs. Right, Maggie?"

Maggie marched straight past the living room without a glance. We could hear her heels on the bare wood floor of the corridor leading to the bedrooms and the sounds of a slammed and locked door.

"Mommy!" Sandi jumped up and followed.

"That's not like Mom. Something must have happened."

"Where was she tonight?" I hesitated to ask. "Out with a man?"

"Oh, Daddy, *please!* She was meeting Nina. They were going to discuss men. You know."

"Yes, Jennifer, I know."

Sandi hadn't returned. We could hear her twisting the doorknob. "Mommy! Come on out. Daddy's here."

"You think something's wrong?" Jennifer beckoned me to follow, but I could not bring myself to go beyond the invisible boundary to the bedrooms. I no longer lived here.

Maggie's voice could be heard telling her daughters to go to bed and she would see them in the morning.

"Are you sure you're okay?" Sandi's voice squeaked with worry. "You want some juice?"

"I'm fine, girls. Just tired. See you in the morning."

Sandi's worry was contagious. "You don't suppose—she's

going to *do* something, do you Dad?" Jennifer likes to put on a melodramatic act, like the world's coming to an end; Sarah Heartburn is what Sonia calls her. Now she wasn't acting. She was genuinely scared. "You know, like pills and stuff?"

"She means suicide, Daddy. Like on TV. And then they find the empty bottle the next morning. Is that what Mommy's going to do?"

"Of course not!" I say, though I'm beginning to have doubts of my own.

I cross the invisible border and tap lightly on the door. "Maggie? It's Dan. The girls have been watching too much television. They think you've locked the door to commit suicide. I know it's silly. You'd never do anything like that. But they love you and they're worried. I'm leaving now, so please open the door and kiss them good night."

What I couldn't tell the girls is that Maggie just didn't want to see me. Sandi hung onto me. "Don't go, Daddy. I thought you were going to stay. Please, Daddy, I need you. I have a headache. I'm sick—"

Jennifer opened the door for me.

"Forget it, Sandi. Daddy doesn't live here anymore."

When I tried to kiss her good night, Sandi shook my hand instead. "I want to thank you for dinner. It was very pleasant."

Back at the hotel, I checked for messages. Liza had not called. When I tried her number, she answered.

"I thought you were going to call me when you got back," I said.

"Shoot me."

"Before you start busting my chops, I want you to know I did not look at sublets tonight. I took my daughters to dinner."

"Good for you. And where was your wife, may I ask?"

"Out—having dinner—I don't know—"

"Well, I do know."

"What's that supposed to mean?"

"Your wife sneaked into my building and scared the shit out of me. She was waiting for me when I got home! Lurking in the hallway outside my apartment!"

"What happened? You sound terrible. I'll be right over."

"No, Dan, please. I'm dead tired. The meeting lasted nearly five hours; they sent out for dinner. I don't want to talk. I just want to sleep."

"Liza, darling. What can I say? I'm so sorry. How dare she do a thing like that! I could wring her neck. Just wait till I speak to her. I have half a mind to call her right this minute."

"No, Dan, take it easy. It's okay. Go to sleep. I'll call you the minute I wake up in the morning."

Liza

I nearly jumped out of my skin. She's lucky I didn't brain her with my tennis racket. Before I knew it, she was gone, down the stairs. I don't know who was more terrified. All I could think of was the rash of recent scorned wife murders: "Scorned Wife Stabs Husband to Death . . . Scorned Wife Shoots Cheating Husband's Mistress . . . Scorned Wife Throws Acid . . . Plants Bomb . . . Slips Poison in Some Chocolates."

Maggie was really only a name before last night, a shadowy figure who had to be dealt with, who I dismissed as having nothing to do with me. I didn't hate her. How could I hate her? I didn't know her. I had often thought it would be convenient if she dropped dead, but that was the kind of wishful thinking you go through when anyone gets in your way. Once, when I was on standby at the Miami airport, trying to get home for Mark's birthday, I had this morbid fantasy that all nine people ahead of me would simultaneously collapse with a tropical fever and be hauled away on stretchers. *Have a good day.*

I can't stop thinking of the anguish in Maggie's face. The woman is in agony. To Dan's credit, he's never put her down, never attacked her the way some married men do. He's simply not in love with her anymore. He's in love with me. He says the marriage has been dead for years. I don't get that impression from her. The woman is in shock. She's not angry because she's losing a meal ticket—she's losing the man she loves.

All I could do was yell down the stairs after her, "I'm sorry—I'm really sorry—I didn't steal your husband—I really didn't—please—believe me—I'm sorry—"

I really don't need this. I've got enough on my plate. The meeting in Connecticut began at 9:00 A.M. with instant coffee in Styrofoam cups and continued without a break until after dark, when they sent out for Chinese food, a veritable medley of slime. It was after ten by the time I got home. I was not in the mood for Dan's wife, and I was not in the mood for Dan when he phoned a while later to ask if he could come over.

At first he didn't—wouldn't—believe me when I told him what happened.

"Maggie would never do anything like that."

"Look, I'm tired."

"She must be very upset."

Am I crazy or did he sound thrilled by the whole thing?

"I'll be right there. We can talk about it."

Didn't he understand English? I wanted to take a hot bath and crawl between cool sheets. I did not want him to come over, and I most certainly did not want to discuss Maggie's emotional problems.

Yesterday's meeting in Connecticut was just the beginning. The deal is set in principle but not signed. I've got a lot on my mind. I've got to bite the bullet and hire two more people.

One of Eileen Ford's bookers sent me her resume last week. If she's still available, that's one. A crazy thought has just crossed my mind. Dan said Maggie is looking for a job. She used to be a model; she'd be perfect. Then it could be like one of those old French films; we'd gang up on Dan and kill him. *Forget it, Manny, it'll never fly.*

I realized a long time ago that there are two kinds of people, complicators and simplifiers. I'm a simplifier. This whole thing is getting too complicated for me. It's Dan's job to simplify. Tonight, I'm going to have it out with him. A divorce is a negotiation. He's got to have a business plan.

I am involved in a furious game of telephone tag with Connecticut, London, Avedon, Athena, and my mother on different lines when Myrna says Sonia is here for our lunch date. It's on my calendar. I've been too busy to look at my calendar. I can't very well cancel now.

Sonia swans in with a million dollars in suede on her body and the kind of jewelry that would bring back Wallis Simpson from the dead. When she lights her cigarette and squints at me through the smoke, she reminds me of Claude Rains's Nazi mother in *Notorious.*

On our way out to Pierre's, I manage to tell Myrna to call me there in half an hour with an emergency that will make it necessary for me to cut lunch short, alas. Time is, after all, money.

Maggie

Dan called first thing this morning.

"I have nothing to say to you, Dan."

"How could you do such a thing, Maggie? How could you go to her house like that?"

"I wanted to see where she lives. I wanted to see the monster. Except she's not a monster. She's just another woman, God help her, and she's in love with you, God help her, though what's so special about you I'm beginning to wonder."

"I wish it didn't have to be like this. I wish you didn't have to be hurt like this."

"Don't flatter yourself. You're not hurting me. I'm hurting myself, but not anymore. You can have your freedom, Dan. I won't fight the divorce. But before you give a sigh of relief, let me tell you now that I do intend to fight for every last penny coming to me and my girls."

"Our girls, Maggie. Remember that."

"I may ask for sole custody—citing Liza as a bad influence on two growing girls."

Dan paused before saying, very quietly, "If you do that, I will tell the court how you hid in Liza's hallway and threatened her life."

So that's the way it's going to be. I was mortified last night, by Nina's behavior and then by my own. But strangely, it's been a catharsis. I feel strong this morning; last night was last night. Today, I'm going to apply for the assistant fashion coordinator job listed in today's *Times*. Tonight, I'm going out on my first date in over fifteen years, with Freddy, for dinner and who knows what afterwards.

Daniel

There's no need to find a sublet. The hotel has given me a larger accommodation at a monthly rate, a small suite with twin beds in the bedroom where the girls can sleep and a sofabed in the living room for me. Not ideal, but okay for the time being. Maggie and I have reached an informal agreement on visitation. Nothing rigid or arbitrary. The girls can stay with me on alternating weekends and a couple of nights during the week, if that's the way it works out. The hotel is nearby, so if they stay over during the week, I can get them to school in the morning.

The Liza thing seems to have blown over. Maggie refuses to discuss it. Liza says we'll talk about it tonight. Sonia has just returned to the office with a cat-that-ate-the-canary look on her face.

"I've just had lunch with Liza. I didn't think you'd mind. Congratulations, Dan. She's one tough cookie. A winner, that girl. A real go-getter, I can tell. She'll be good for our business, mark my words. Not like Maggie."

"Sonia, get one thing straight. I will not hear a word against Maggie, not one word. Do I make myself clear?" I keep thinking of her hiding in Liza's doorway, and all because of me. It breaks my heart.

At five o'clock I call the girls for our daily phone date.

The first thing Jennifer says is, "Guess what, Dad? Mommy's got a boyfriend."

Liza

Ever since he left home, it's been downhill. We talked for hours last night, going over the same territory again and again and *again,* till I wanted to scream. What's to discuss? Either he gets the divorce or he doesn't. Either we get married or we don't. I'm getting tired of the whole thing. I would be one lousy diplomat. I read about peace negotiations here, treaty negotiations there, the United Nations in New York, Geneva on the lake—what do they talk about all day for months on end? Who says what, and who disagrees, and what do they actually say during all those endless discussions? Or is it all sound and fury, signifying nothing?

At least Dan and I are hot for each other. There is something very mysterious about attraction. The fact is, we *fit,* and not just sexually, though you can't knock that. We're right for each other, we're cozy together. When I'm with him, it's sanguine. I don't want to lose him. When I'm working, it's something else. I can put him in a little compartment and shut the door and get on with things, content in the knowledge that he's there.

I hate the idea that somebody's got to get hurt. Last time around, it was me. It took me months to get over it. This time it's Maggie. I feel for her, but it can't be helped. Nothing comes free. If you want happiness, you've got to pay for it. If you want success, you've got to pay for that, too.

In more ways than one. Sonia said, "So you're the notorious Liza!" like it was a compliment. She was admiring me for being ruthless. I would have liked hearing that once upon a time, when I worried about being perceived as a pushover, when I wanted to intimidate people and make them afraid of me. Now I wasn't so sure. Why isn't it possible to win without someone else losing?

Mark's reaction is the same. Our relationship has dwindled down to an occasional cocktail. When I told him about Dan, he went all peculiar, kind of goofy and reverent at the same time. "I can't tell you how much I respect you, Liza." He said it with the adoring puppy dog look of someone meeting a movie star.

"You mean because I'm a homewrecker? Does that make me more glamorous, a more valuable person?"

"It means you're strong. You know what you want and you take it. I should never have let you go."

Myrna, too, seems overly excited by the fact that a man left his wife and children for me. Irini, too, and Athena—all of them treating me like a heroine, grinning at me with fascination, like I've *done* something. It reminds me of my brief career as a groupie with a saxophone player in a jazz quartet. I went on gigs with him, riding with the band in the van, sitting with the wives and girlfriends where the fans could see us and speculate over who was whose girl. I thought it was glamorous to be pointed at and envied. I enjoyed watching girls come on to my man, slip notes in his pocket and rub against him, knowing he was mine and that after each set, he would sit with me.

What a crock. The thrill of it all wore off soon enough. I didn't need the envy of strangers to validate my appeal. I don't want it now. I hate the thought of people wondering what I've got between my legs to break up Dan's marriage. I want them to admire me and respect me for what I've got between my ears.

Brains, dammit. And integrity. I'll have to be careful to see that this divorce doesn't boomerang on my reputation. A man can leave his wife, and nobody questions his business morals.

But the woman who's involved is considered suspect and emotionally unstable, so how can you trust her judgment?

My throat hurts, dammit. I can't afford to have a cold right now. Or ever. I've got too much to do.

Maggie

Jennifer was waiting up for me when I got home from my date with Freddy. I was trying to decide whether to tiptoe him down the hall to my bedroom when Jennifer stumbled out of hers, pretending to sleepwalk. The act was so transparent, we both had to laugh. I think Freddy was as relieved as I was. We had trapped ourselves into the situation, flirting outrageously, Freddy doing his Stanley Kowalski imitation—"We've had this date from the very beginning."

"You busy this weekend?" he asked before kissing me on the cheek.

"Call me," I commanded, hoping to impress my teenage daughter with my power over men.

"What's the big idea!" she said when he left.

"What big idea?"

"You know goddam well—"

"Jennifer, I will not have you use that kind of language!"

"You do know what I mean. You were taking him into Daddy's bed."

"Jennifer—you are the daughter. I am the mother. I'm supposed to wait up for you. What I do is none of your business."

"It *is* my business. You're my mother."

"My bedroom is *my* bedroom. It is no longer your father's bedroom. He no longer lives here. Can't you get that through your head? The marriage is over. I am now a single woman and I have been out on a date."

"Did you go back to Freddy's place?"

"Jennifer, I'm warning you."

"Well, did you?"

The idiocy of the conversation hit us both simultaneously. We fell into each other's arms, shrieking with laughter.

"Did you, Mom, did you?"

"No, Jennifer, I did not." In a mock baby voice, I added, "Mommy was a good girl!" and laughter engulfed us again.

I've heard that at a certain point mothers and daughters stop being adversaries and become friends. I hoped this was the start of the good times for Jennifer and me. It was like being back at college and telling my roommate about my date.

Jennifer wanted to hear every detail of the evening—where we went, what we ate.

"Your mother kicked a jukebox to death!"

She sat at my feet with her elbows on my knees and her face propped up on her fists, as if I were telling a fairy tale. In a way, I suppose it was—the princess imprisoned for years out on her first date. With impeccable instinct, Freddy had chosen the noisiest place on Columbus Avenue. The music was so loud, it was impossible to talk. To order a drink, you had to write it down on the waiter's pad. I wrote: "Can you please turn the jukebox down?" The waiter replied, "That's the way the manager wants it."

On my way to the ladies room, I passed the jukebox. It was so loud, it vibrated. On my way back, on a sudden impulse, I kicked it as hard as I could. The sound stopped abruptly. Patrons cheered. "Right on!" But my triumph was short-lived. An extremely short, fat man plowed through the crowd with his fists raised.

"I'm sorry. I'll pay the damages."

Freddy appeared at my side. "It's okay. She's had a few."

The manager punched his fist into the palm of his other hand.

"You're one lucky broad."

Reaching down, he reconnected the plug I had dislodged with my kick and the music started up. People patted us and offered to buy us drinks as we made our way back to our table.

"I think this is enough excitement for one night," I told Freddy. Walking home, I had to admit to feeling turned on by the run-in, the touch of danger. Freddy felt it, too. "You were wonderful, Maggie." We kissed on the street, and when we got home we'd have gone to bed if Jennifer hadn't gone into her sleepwalking act.

But I was glad she'd interrupted. Freddy could wait. Either we'd do it or we wouldn't. At this moment I was enjoying my daughter. It had been quite a full day in other respects.

"I went on a job interview this morning. At Saks Fifth Avenue. They're looking for an assistant to the fashion coordinator, someone with modeling experience to help put on fashion shows."

"You'd be perfect, Mom. Did you tell them you were a famous model? What happened? When do you start? Wait till I tell Dad."

"They said I was perfect for the job, but to be fair, they had to interview the other applicants." What they actually said was to come back in two weeks for the final round of interviews.

Something else happened in Saks that really shook me and made me realize I'm not as together as I think I am, and that I'd better take care of myself if I don't want to crack up. After the interview, I decided to look at scarves. It was crowded on the main floor. I had worn my cashmere cape to impress the personnel woman. Now, I was overwhelmed with its hotness and took it off. After a while, unable to make a choice, I decided to leave. With my cape in place and my gloves on, I reached for my handbag, only to find it was gone.

It had been on the counter a second ago. The saleswoman searched through the scarves. The security officer rushed over at her signal. "It was right here!" It had everything in it—keys, wallet, cash, credit cards, pictures of Dan and the girls, the expensive gold compact he'd given me that I never used but thought would also impress the interviewer in case I needed it. All gone!

At last there was nothing to do but go upstairs to file a report. Everyone was extremely attentive. Would I like some coffee? Did I need some cash to get home? There was a telephone to call my husband if I so required. It was hot in the little cubicle. When I threw back my cape, there was my handbag. What I had done when I finished looking at scarves was to automatically sling my bag over my shoulder and put my cape on over that.

"Happens all the time," they assured me. "Don't worry about it."

I was worried, though. I am worried. I departed the store with as much dignity as I could muster. Why should a lousy job interview so unnerve me? But it wasn't just the job interview, it was everything—the divorce, having a date, remembering Nina and that horrible episode with Liza. On top of everything else, I nearly killed myself running down those fire exit stairs. I tripped over a pail on one of the landings and went flying. Fortunately, I've got good coordination and grabbed onto the bannister to save myself.

From now on, I'll have to do more than that to save myself.

There's another problem I have to face. When I left Saks, I looked frantically for the nearest bar, Charley O's, and I ordered a drink, a double vodka on the rocks.

Daniel

My lawyer wants to know what kind of a settlement I have in mind, how much alimony I think Maggie would accept, what sorts of trust funds and insurance I want to set up for the girls. I don't know what to say. How should I know what Maggie needs to run the house? He's the lawyer, he should be telling me what he thinks I should do.

"I just want to be fair."

"That's what every man says, till it comes down to the nitty-gritty."

"Why don't you ask Maggie's lawyer what she has in mind?"

"That is not how to negotiate a divorce."

I wouldn't know. I've heard enough men mouthing off about their ex-wives having them by the short and curlies. I remember one guy who quit his job and went to jail rather than pay alimony. "I worked my balls off for ten years so she could take dance classes. Let her get a job as a dancing teacher." The last I heard he'd disappeared.

Maggie's different from other women. She's sweet and considerate, an old-fashioned homemaker. One of the things that bothers me is how square she is; a one-man woman, she's always said, and I'm the one man she's loved. That doesn't make me feel too swift. She's still young and still beautiful. I hate to think of her living like a nun, devoting herself solely to the home and the children. That may be what she prefers. I can't really see her at singles bars. Jennifer's trying to make me jealous, I know. *Mommy's got a boyfriend!* The little witch.

"Is it true, Maggie? Jennifer says you have a boyfriend." We're discussing the girls' weekend.

"Is that what she told you?"

"Come on, Maggie, you can tell me. Has somebody come along and swept you off your feet?"

"Why do you want to know?" This isn't what I expect. I expect her to say don't be silly, Jennifer's exaggerating as usual.

Why do I want to know? Good question. "I want to know because if you get married again, I won't have to pay alimony."

"Don't count on it, Dan."

"You mean you are seeing someone?"

"What's so amazing about it? You may treat me like the Virgin Mary, but I'm not. You have a lover, why shouldn't I?"

"That's different. You have the children. What will they think?"

For the first time in her life, Maggie uses what she primly refers to as "the F-word": "If their father can fuck around, so can their mother." I can hear the hysteria in her voice.

"Let's drop it, shall we? You're absolutely right. I have no right to interfere in your private life. Tell me about the job at Saks."

"Oh, that. I'll know in another ten days or so. But, Dan dear—"

"Yes, Maggie dear!"

"Don't think my getting a job is going to lower my alimony. You've heard the Divorced Wife's Golden Rule, haven't you? 'She who gets the gold rules.'"

Liza

I've been wanting to meet the girls, to start getting to know them. But Dan says it's too soon, they'll feel disloyal to Maggie. We'd better just leave it in abeyance for the time being.

We seem to be in limbo. I've stopped nagging him about a sublet. If he's happy in that dumb hotel, that's his business. We see each other almost every night. I don't ask about the divorce proceedings. He doesn't volunteer.

We're settling into a routine. I love him more than any other man, with the possible exception of Mark. I love being with him, and if anything our sex life is better than ever. But if I'm being honest, I'd rather not rock the boat. I'm beginning to think I need to live alone. I need privacy when I'm burned out. One Sunday when he had the children, I stayed in bed all day with the shades drawn and the answering machine on. I had planned to clean out the bathroom closet, throw away dead makeup, and work on the needlepoint I began two years ago.

I watched movies and drifted in and out of sleep. The only times I got up were to go to the bathroom and to get a dish of ice cream.

My Connecticut deal is in its final stages of nit-picking. Meantime, the letter of intent has started the machinery at full speed. Eileen Ford's ex-booker is a human dynamo. She's funny. She says my operation is positively pastoral compared to Eileen's. At my shop, she has time to pee.

Dan appears resigned to my London trip. I'll be away ten days, possibly longer if I take Chelsea Britt to Paris.

"I'll miss you, darling."

"I'll miss you, too."

"Aren't you worried about leaving me alone in the big, bad city?" I hate it when he's being cute.

"And why should I be worried, Dan?"

"Well—I don't know—I might get lonely—and go back to Maggie!"

"Is that a threat?"

"No, Liza—of course not! I was only teasing. Can't you take a joke? I want the divorce more than ever. Honest. And by the time you get back, I'll have some definite news. Honest."

Meantime, I have something new to worry about.

Daniel

The night before Liza was to leave for London, she was more preoccupied than I've ever seen her.

"What is it, Liza? Tell me. Maybe I can help."

"It's nothing. The trip. It's going to mean a lot."

Every trip means a lot, every deal is the most important. I've got a business, too. I get excited about developing new clients, too. Maybe by this time I'm jaded, or at least I'm not obsessed the way she is.

"Maybe I'll go back to the hotel. I know how you get before a big trip." Lists, folders, photographs, and tearsheets were all over the place. Liza's idea of packing light is to dump her entire wardrobe on the floor and pick out one by one the absolute basics she will need. Every surface in the apartment was covered. I know she didn't mean it, but I felt very much in the way.

"I guess I should get some sleep. The limo's picking me up at eight for the ten o'clock flight."

"I'll miss you, Liza."

"I'll miss you, too."

The words sounded oddly mechanical. She walked me to the door, opened it with a theatrical flourish, and then abruptly slammed it shut. "Dan, there's something I've got tell you. I thought it could keep till I got back, but it can't."

Now I know why she's been so twitchy the last few days, I thought. She wants to check out and doesn't know how. I felt a faint stirring of relief. This living in limbo has been getting to me. I see other men getting divorced all the time. It doesn't seem to bother them. I don't know how they do it. I've been going quietly nuts. I have pains in my chest. It's wearing me down. Sonia thinks I may be getting an ulcer. That's all I need.

"What is it, Liza? Have you decided to ditch me and marry Mark?"

"You really can be the pits sometimes. Why do you joke about everything? This is no joke, Dan. I'm pretty sure I'm pregnant."

Most definitely, it was not a joke. I was at a loss for words. "What are you going to do?" I realized I'd said "you," not "we," not "What are *we* going to do?"

You don't have to draw diagrams for Liza. She understood the implication. "That's really the point, isn't it? I'll throw the ball back into your court. What do *you* want me to do?"

A straight question deserves a straight answer. Do I want her to have our baby, or don't I? The idea of a second family at my age is something I can't take lightly. If it's a girl, I'd be over sixty-five when she finished college, the oldest geezer at graduation.

We agreed to a moratorium while Liza's away, almost two

weeks to think about what we want to do. When she gets back, we'll decide.

Maggie

Liza's in England on business. Dan suggested I join them when he took the girls out to dinner. I made a counter suggestion: Why didn't he have dinner at home with us? It would be much nicer than going to a restaurant.

Wouldn't I mind? Dan asks.

"Why should I mind? You're paying the bills. It will be nice for Jennifer and Sandi to have you visit. Civilized."

"I just don't think it's right."

Poor guy. He didn't worry about cheating on his wife, and now he thinks he's cheating on his girlfriend by having dinner here with me and the kids. I should worry. The fact is, I'd rather eat my own cooking in my own dining room.

The girls seem to be adjusting to the situation. They are watching the six o'clock news with Dan, laughing and talking back to the screen, when a special report shows runaway children near the Port Authority. Two girls about Jennifer and Sandi's age were found panhandling commuters. Where did they sleep? "In doorways."

Sandi bursts into tears and buries her face in Dan's chest. Jennifer is crying, too. "It's okay, Sandi, that won't happen to us. We won't have to sleep in doorways, will we?"

At this moment, I feel sorrier for him than I have ever felt for another human being. The poor son of a bitch. It serves him right.

Liza

Ah, to be in England! I threw a little reception at the Chelsea Town Hall as a way of introducing Chelsea Britt to the media. The popular press was amused by the notion, as one reporter put it, of naming a model girl after a London borough. One of the more argumentative papers sent a political correspondent to interview me—a Michael Caine clone, circa *Alfie.*

It was something of a standoff. He was trying to get me to comment on the Stealth Bomber, as well as America's morbid obsession with the Royal Family. I was trying to stick to the subject of modeling and beauty—the reason I'm in London—by voicing my profound professional admiration for Princess Diana.

"She has The Look," is what I said, and what the front-page headline cried. "It's too bad she married Prince Charles. I'd have signed her up with Liza Central and turned her into a supermodel," is what I said. It came out: "Cheeky Liza Wants Di as Supermodel."

"Would cheeky Liza like to buy me a drink now that I've made her famous?"

"Men generally buy me drinks."

So far, the trip has been a hands-down success professionally. Chelsea Britt is booked for three covers of *Harper's Queen* and twelve editorial pages called "Chelsea in Chelsea" for *Vogue.* Several top British manufacturers attended the reception. I've had belly-to-belly meetings in my hotel suite for three days running.

The personal front is less promising—not a word from Dan, not a flower cabled from New York, not a miss-you note or a telephone call. My other situation, to put it as delicately as possible, remains unchanged. I think wistfully of how often in the past air travel has brought on my period, an unexpected and unwanted intrusion on my plans, particularly when they included a man.

This time, wouldn't you know it, the flight was smooth as silk, the descent as gentle as velvet. I could have balanced a glass of champagne on my head without spilling a drop.

My newspaper friend has patiently pursued. Phone calls. A bottle of champagne. An invitation to a private viewing of new acquisitions at the Tate, which I'd have given my eyeteeth to attend but couldn't because of—"I know, business!" he chorused over the phone.

This morning, he called bright and early with the cryptic message, "I'm collecting you tonight at seven. Be here."

It's Friday. All of London is heading for the countryside. Chelsea Britt is visiting relatives in Gloucestershire until we fly to Paris Sunday night. I am in the trough after riding the crest of the wave all week.

The phone rings at seven precisely. Good sign. I like a man who comes when he says he's going to come—bad sign. Or maybe it's a good bad sign. When I feel as horny as I feel now, it means only one thing—I'm about to get my period.

We start out at pubs, graduate to clubs, and wind up at Annabel's in Berkeley Square—no nightingales, thank you very much. It occurs to me this guy is spending money like there's no tomorrow. Either he's spending his entire week's salary to impress me like a Somerset Maugham story, or he's a duke or lord disguised as a Fleet Street hack.

As it turns out, he's on an expense account and is house-sitting a mews house off Belgrave Square for a tax refugee living in Dublin.

"Hope you don't mind. I've got to walk the dogs. Their little bladders must be bursting."

The interior of the little house is a time warp of silver and portraits and leatherbound books and sofas with tassels. I could be happy here, at least for the next few hours.

"Let me show you the gardens."

Only residents have a key to the Belgrave Square Gardens. Once inside, the dogs are released and run off in all directions with yelps of ecstasy. There are no lights in the gardens. The undergrowth is thick, the shrubs and bushes dense as a forest primeval. "Now," is all he says, more than making up for the twit I met on the plane from California.

Later, as we have brandies under a portrait of Lord Kitchener, I describe how the man stripped down to nothing but a smug smile. "You see, you have restored the honor of all Englishmen."

"Oh, you Americans. Can't you tell?"

What have I done now?

"I'm Irish, you silly cow."

Daniel

I know I should have called her. She expected me to call her. She gave me all the hotel numbers—phone, telex, and Fax. Not that she had to bother. She knows I've got all the listings at the office. I thought about it every damned day. It's hard to explain. I don't understand it myself. I simply could not bring myself to do it.

She's been gone two weeks. It seems like a year, and at the same time it seems like ten minutes, like she just left. I haven't had time to think. What's she doing back so soon?

"How did everything go?"

"Fine. They loved Chelsea Britt. They loved me, too. My picture in the paper. Fabulous."

"Nothing else to report?"

"If you mean am I still pregnant, the answer is yes."

"Liza, darling. I'm so happy. I love you so much." As the words tumble out, I realize I mean them. I didn't realize how much I've missed her until I heard her voice.

This settles it. The divorce must go through as quickly as possible. I won't tell the girls about the baby just yet, but I think it's time for them to meet Liza and get to know her before she starts showing and they really freak out.

We'll do it this Saturday. At my place, the hotel; it's neutral territory but familiar to them so they'll feel secure. They'll sleep over Friday night. Liza will come over on Saturday afternoon. Before you know it, they'll all be friends.

Maggie

I didn't know she was back. I should have guessed from the way the girls were acting on Friday night, whispering and *shhh*-ing each other when I passed by their room. I thought they were feeling guilty about spending the night with Dan. I tried to make it easy for them, to show them I didn't feel betrayed.

"Daddy will be here any minute. You're going to have a wonderful time."

Dan had joined us for dinner three times in Liza's absence.

He seemed so relaxed and happy with Liza away. We were a family again, couldn't he see that? Each time, I prayed that he would stay. Each time, I was sure in my heart that he wanted to, that he didn't want to go back to the hotel. I begged him silently to gather the three of us into his arms and say, "I'm home to stay."

It was a pipe dream. On Saturday night when he brought the girls back, Dan did not come up as he usually did. They were alone when they got off the elevator.

"Where's Daddy?"

"He's—he's with—" Sandi looked stricken.

"With Liza, Mom. We met Liza." Jennifer stood her ground, but I could see she was also frightened.

"It's all right, girls. Don't worry. It's fine." It wasn't their fault; it was Dan's. How dare he introduce them to Liza without my knowledge or permission!

But I couldn't let my anger get the best of me. I had to find out what happened.

"Did she bring you presents?"

The girls exchanged guilty glances.

"It's *okay.* You can tell me. I won't be angry."

Liza had given them each a fashion wristwatch that could also be worn as a pin or a belt buckle.

I struggled to keep the sarcasm from my voice—and the annoyance. "Just what you wanted, right? She knows what girls like, right? It's a good thing you've told me. I was going to buy them for you myself."

In a burst of shared confidences, Sandi explained, "It was Daddy's idea. Liza said she asked Daddy what he thought we wanted and he said the watches, that she could get us off his back if she bought us the watches."

"Well, now—let's see how they look."

Back to the guilty looks. Dan had suggested they leave their gifts behind at the hotel, so as not to upset me. The bastard was making me sound like a witch. What did he think I would do, rip the watches off their wrists?

Control. Control.

"That's silly. Tell Daddy it's very nice of Liza to give you things. You don't have to hide anything from me."

Having reassured them, I then had to listen with a loving, smiling face as they described the afternoon with Liza. There was a line a mile long outside the Hard Rock Cafe; Liza knew the manager and got them right in. Afterwards, they went to the renovated Children's Zoo in Central Park.

"Do you know what Liza can do?" Sandi was bursting to tell me.

"What?"

"She can jump over a bench."

Jennifer chimed in. "You should see her. She runs down the hill and leaps over the bench! Weird."

Something I can't do. Maybe next time she'll break her neck.

"Did Daddy do it, too?"

"Moth-er—Dad's too old for that!"

"I hope you girls didn't try anything as dangerous as that."

Good old square Mommy, at it again.

"Well, now. So what did you think of her?"

More of those looks.

"She's okay."

"Do you think she's pretty?"

"Not as pretty as you, Mom. Nobody's as pretty as you!"

Both my daughters flung their arms around their poor old mother.

Liza

I felt like I was on trial. Sandi was easy, a real cuddler. She's like me, she can't get enough hugs. Jennifer was something else. She shook hands with me when Dan introduced us. He was nervous, too.

"Give Liza a kiss."

"No, Dan. Jennifer's right. We've only just met. Shaking hands is fine. I hope we'll get to be friends. Then maybe we'll get around to kissing."

The idea of the wristwatches was inspired. Dan said they'd been pestering him for weeks. I didn't want to arrive loaded down like Santa Claus. I wanted just the right thing. Sandi danced around the room with pleasure. Jennifer put hers on with a succinct "Thanks."

"Now, doesn't Liza deserve a kiss?" Dan prompted.

"Not at all, Dan. I'm just glad the girls like them." Quit pushing, Dan. This is hard on them. Let them get used to me.

"Tell them about the modeling business. Jennifer wants to be a model."

They listened to my stories about Athena and Chelsea Britt and the others. I was just warming up to my task when Jennifer cut me short. "I'm hungry."

Dan upbraided her for being rude. I jumped in again, saying I was hungry, too. I made extra points getting us into the Hard Rock Cafe and hit Olympic stride when I took that flying leap over the bench. It wasn't all to show-off—I thought this might bring on my period.

After we dropped the girls home, Dan and I had our first real talk since my return from England. The magic was still there, no doubt about it.

"I missed you, Liza. I tried to put you out of my mind. I even had dinner with Maggie and the girls at home to see how I felt, whether I wanted to go back. I don't, darling. I want you. I know I've been a bastard. I don't know what's wrong with me. I thought of you every day. I wanted to call you. I just couldn't. And now, with the baby and all, it's settled. We'll be married as soon as I get the divorce."

And what progress had he made in that particular area?

"Don't worry. These things take time. The lawyer says he's working on it."

We're back the way we were. I've put my anger and resentments aside. I'm committed to this man. And this baby, too. Jumping over that bench was asinine. I've lost one baby. Having a baby isn't all that simple. The circumstances may not be perfect. With lawyers the way they are, I may give birth before we can get married. Rosalind will have a fit. But so be it. I'm happy. I had an express letter from my Belgrave Square lothario. He'll be in New York next month and would like to see me. But that part of my life is over. I'm going to get married and have a baby—in no particular order.

It was a perfect Sunday afternoon for the park. We'd finished the puzzle and decided to take a walk. It's strange how our lives have centered on this park—Central Park, well-named. The city would die without it. I suppose what happened next was inevitable.

We were strolling arm-in-arm, sharing a Dove bar and approaching the Alice-in-Wonderland sculpture north of the miniature boat basin, when there they were coming toward us. Maggie stood stone-faced, as if daring us to come one step further. Maggie clutched the girls' hands as if we were the Gestapo come to take them away.

Dan was struck dumb. He held out his arms to his daughters. They clung to their mother. I found myself talking very fast, as I always do when I'm caught unawares, chattering away about what a pretty day and isn't it lucky the predictions of rain turned out to be wrong and how the weather reporters don't know what they're talking about.

During the ghastly pause that followed, Maggie said, "I want to thank you for the lovely gifts, Liza. It was very thoughtful of you. The girls are writing you thank-you notes."

Jennifer was peering intently at me while pretending not to. She was wearing her hair frizzed out, with one chandelier earring; there were about a hundred badges and pins on her sweatshirt.

I addressed myself to Maggie. "How pretty Jennifer looks today. Dan tells me she'd like to be a model. All fathers think their daughters are beautiful, but I think Jennifer may have what it takes. Maybe sometime soon, I can arrange for some test shots."

"So that's it. My husband isn't enough. Now you want my children, too!"

The excitement on Jennifer's face turned to pain. She realized she had nearly been disloyal to Maggie. "I want you to know my mother was a model—a famous model—and she's a lot prettier than you'll ever be!"

Maggie

Was it my imagination? She looked pregnant; there was something about her breasts. First thing Monday morning, I called Dan and got straight to the point. "Is Liza pregnant?"

They weren't absolutely sure, was all he could say.

I had a million things to do, but I was paralyzed. A letter had arrived from Saks Fifth Avenue, saying they had deferred the new fashion show program for six months and would be in touch. I canceled out on my neighborhood beautification patrol. The trees would have to get along without me. I cut my ceramics class and left poor little Sandi to the mercies of the other mothers who were taking her group to the Museum of Natural History in the afternoon.

I couldn't bring myself to get dressed. What difference did it make? I poured some vodka in my orange juice, and when that was gone, I poured some more into the orange juice glass. Oblivion is what I wanted. I must have dozed off on the couch, still in my nightgown, when the ringing doorbell penetrated the fog. *Daniel.* What I must look like! I would say I'd taken sick—food poisoning, that was it.

The window-washer strode in, dressed cowboy-style in jeans and boots, an apparition of shoulders, chest, hair, and tattoos, and impatient to get started. I dimly remembered having called Flatiron to make the arrangements.

"Where do you want me to start? I ain't got all day."

I was mortified by my appearance. It must have been noon, and there I was like Blanche du Bois, barefoot in a faded nightgown, my hair all over the place. "This way."

My chief thought was to get to my bedroom and dress while he started with the kitchen. I must have tripped, because the next thing I knew I was on the floor and he was hauling me to my feet—"You okay, lady?"—which was precisely the moment Jennifer returned from school.

"Mother! How could you!"

Why was she shouting at me? Why did the window-washer leave without doing the windows? Don't they know I like my house to be immaculate, but that I wasn't feeling very well?

"No wonder Daddy left you for another woman!"

Daniel

There's no other way. I've got to take charge of the situation. If I don't, who will? I've never seen Maggie like this, her nightgown stained, her head lolling like one of those bag ladies in Grand Central Station. Jennifer was scared out of her mind, poor kid. I've got to hand it to her. She's got her head screwed on. She called me at the office and got Maggie into bed somehow.

"I'm sorry, Dan." It was all she could say.

I'm sorry, too, Maggie, so deeply sorry that I don't love you anymore.

She was asleep when the doctor got there. Sandi was home by then. Jennifer became the mother before my very eyes. She gave Sandi her milk and graham crackers and escorted her to her room to do her homework. As a mark of consideration, she allowed Sandi to leave the bedroom door open instead of shut, as Maggie always insists on for study time.

Dr. Minkow phoned a prescription for a tranquilizer to the drugstore. "Just to help her to rest the next few days. I don't want her to become dependent on them. The alcohol dependency is the danger. Fortunately for her, she can't consume too much. She passes out."

He didn't say it, but I could tell he blamed it on me. He mentioned therapy as something for serious discussion. The sooner, the better. "Maggie's in bad trouble, Dan. What happened today is a cry for help."

I hope Liza will understand. If she loves me the way she says she does, she will. She'll postpone our happiness for a while. We've got everything—each other, our love, a baby on the way. Maggie has nothing. We've taken her life away from her. We've got to think of somebody besides ourselves.

I found the letter from Saks Fifth Avenue on the kitchen table. Another rejection. My heart breaks for her. For Jennifer, too. The poor kid is beside herself with remorse. She told me what she said to Maggie. "I didn't mean it, Daddy! Tell her I didn't mean it. I'm sorry. How could I say such a rotten thing to my own mother? Why can't things be the way they used to?"

Liza didn't say too much when I called her. What could she say? "I have no choice. Maggie is having a breakdown. She and the children need me. I'm moving back in tonight. I'll stay as long as I have to stay."

Liza's response was threefold: She was sorry. She was in a meeting. She'd speak to me later.

Liza

It's blackmail. The tyranny of the weak. No contest. The weak shall inherit the earth. The pathetic shall win by losing. I can predict the entire scenario: This time, it's vodka. Next time, it's pills. Maybe a little nick on the wrists. A little note taped on a locked bedroom door. There's no way I can compete with that.

I feel sorry for Dan. He's in pain. He can't see the trap he's in. I believe him when he says he's only moving back temporarily. It's an emergency. His family needs him. He has no choice. What would I have him do, hire an outsider?

I believe him when he says he loves me. I love him, but there's no way I'm going to live my life in another woman's soap opera.

I tell him I do understand his dilemma. He has my sympathy. He has my love. He also has exactly one month from today to start the divorce.

"Is that an ultimatum?" How can I act this way when he's got so much on his plate!

I assure him, with all my sympathy and love, that it is indeed an ultimatum.

While I still have the courage of my convictions, I call Mark and ask if he'd like to have dinner.

"I need a friend, Mark."

"You can always count on me."

I'm glad Mark's free tonight. It's been ages since I've seen him. Old husbands are the best husbands, I always say. I can relax with him. I can tell him everything. How I met Dan. Falling in love. Our plans to marry.

"You met him, Mark. What did you think?"

"One hell of a classy-looking guy."

"That's what I think. There are problems, of course. Aren't there always problems. But, Mark—I'm going to have a baby!"

Involuntarily, he makes a face.

"Say something, Mark. Congratulate me. Tell me I'm crazy, I don't care. I'm pregnant. You know, baby makes three!"

He says that after giving up on me, he started dating a psychiatrist, Vanessa. She's wonderful, the best thing that ever happened to him. She's straightening out his life.

"She knows what went wrong with our marriage."

"And how does she know that?"

"I told her all about it. You, me, the baby, Tiffany. Everything. She says the mind controls the body, and that's why you lost the baby. You really didn't want the baby. You really didn't want to be married—to me or anyone else—and when you caught me in bed with Tiffany, you jumped at it. Your big chance to be free."

"Let me understand this. According to Vanessa, I arranged for you to screw Tiffany in my bed so I could catch you and use it as an excuse to get a divorce?"

"If it hadn't been Tiffany, it'd have been some other excuse. If you'd wanted to save our marriage, we'd have worked it out."

"That's a fascinating concept. You destroy the marriage; it's up to me to save it."

"Face the facts, Liza. You don't want a husband. You want money and power. That's why you've picked Dan, a married man who's never going to get a divorce, and that'll be another excuse to stay free."

"You told Vanessa about Dan?"

"I tell Vanessa everything."

"How would Vanessa feel if I invited you home to bed?"

He laughs. "That's what she said you might do. You'd love her, Liza. She said a lot of formerly marrieds have affairs after the divorce. The sexual attraction is still there. Take us, for example. We know each other's bodies, our sexual tastes. We know from experience how to turn each other on, what we like, what we don't like. Like I told Vanessa, we were great sexual partners. We learned from our mistakes and from each other. So why shouldn't we enjoy each other again?"

"Let me be sure I understand. Your friend, Vanessa, the psychiatrist, wouldn't mind your spending the night with me?"

"She says it's all part of personal growth. She says I have a long way to go."

She can say that again.

"Did you tell her about the slow strip you used to like me to do?"

"She thinks that's fabulous. You are truly a remarkable woman."

"And the ketchup? You didn't forget the ketchup?"

He looked perplexed.

"I don't remember any ketchup."

"You must have passed out from the excitement."

Do all ex-husbands become less than strangers? It's hard to believe I once actually lived with this man and had intimate knowledge of his body.

He brings me home. I haven't made up my mind whether I want to add a new chapter to Vanessa's research. There's a message from Dan on my machine. He's thinking of me. The girls send their love. Maggie is resting comfortably.

I'll bet she is.

I've lost interest, if I ever really had any interest, in putting Mark through his paces.

"Thanks for listening, Mark. You're a good friend. I hope you won't mind if I ask you to run along."

"Vanessa said that's exactly what you'd do. Lead me on to prove you could still do it—and drop me like a hot potato."

I am wondering if Vanessa has discovered his habit of farting in bed, or his tendency toward premature ejaculation.

Alone at last with my career, I am distressed to find I have forgotten to bring home a bag of banknotes to play with. I turn on the television. The programs seem evenly divided between kissing and killing. They're having fun and I'm not.

I think of the men I've known before and since Mark. I thought I knew Mark. Clearly, I didn't. Other men I've known even less. I've never considered myself especially promiscuous, but there've been a hell of a lot of good times. The best times were the adventures, the crazy times abroad. London. Paris. Cannes. Milano. Rome. Corfu. Athens. A Baedeker of romance with foreign men with foreign habits in foreign beds.

Foreign men smell better than American men. Sweat. Garlic. Liniment. Cologne so strong it makes your eyes tear—preferable to deodorants, especially when it comes to armpits. I wonder if Mark told Vanessa I like armpits.

Following the divorce, the men's faces blur. There was one I nicknamed the repeater rifle. Another insisted on taking me to a motel. He was divorced. I was divorced. We each had an apartment; but no, he could only perform well in a motel room. I'd love to know Vanessa's theory about that. I've got a pretty good idea: Sex is good, but it isn't nice—ipso—and facto, a sleazy motel. I get it but I don't get it.

My favorite trip down Memory Lane is the time I had three different men in three different countries in a twenty-four-hour period. I had been staying with Enzo in Sardinia. Early one morning he flew me in his Cessna to the Nice airport, where an old friend, Jean-Paul, had offered to pick me up and drive me to Paris if I'd pay for the fuel. Halfway to Paris, we stopped for a *picnique* in a shaded grove. One thing led to another, and we just made it to Le Bourget for my nine o'clock flight to London, where Simon was waiting for me in his houseboat on the Chelsea Embankment.

It was like climbing Annapurna, something you only do once and remember the rest of your life.

An old campaigner at thirty-two, that's what I am, remembering the glory days and grateful I had them. All women should sow their wild oats when they're young. It does them more good than it does men. Men think they're getting away with something; women know they're getting onto something—a subtle but sublime difference.

Riffling through the *Times,* I see an ad: "Men . . . Sale."

Halfway asleep, I amuse myself with the speculation about how much one would cost, a custom-made man tailored to my personal specifications. But what if I ordered one and he didn't fit?

If I lose Dan, if he stays with Maggie, I may just decide to have my baby and forget about sex. On balance, I've been lucky. Nobody has ever beaten me up or date-raped me or stolen my jewelry. From what I see of the current scene, I'm basically too old-fashioned. I close my eyes when I make love. Not from shame, but for courtesy's sake.

Obviously, I will need escorts for my professional and social commitments. New York is a storehouse of men delighted to be invited anywhere but bed. *Round up the usual rejects.*

Maggie

I'm holding my breath, fingers crossed. Dan has been an angel. Nothing is too much for him to do. The first few days, he came home for lunch with chicken soup from the deli—Jewish penicillin, good for what ails you. "And if nothing ails you, it's good for that, too!" he said. He spoon-fed me. Brushed my hair. Told me not to worry about some dumb little job at Saks. He and Sonia have some friends in the fashion world. When I'm up on my feet, he says, they'll find me a good job where I can use all of my talents—and my looks.

I asked Helen why I had to fall on my face for people to offer a helping hand. It's the way of the world, she said. Did I want her to come East? I was fine, I assured her, and getting better every day. Did I want her to have a nice friendly talk with Dan? I said he was being so wonderful, I didn't want to rock the boat.

"He said it would be temporary, Helen, until I got on my feet. He's kept the hotel room. He sees Liza, the girls tell me that, but he's back here early every night."

"Does he sleep with you?"

"He's not that wonderful. But he stays with me, reading or watching television until I fall asleep. Oh, Helen, I haven't been this happy in years. How can I get him to move back permanently?"

"You could have a relapse."

"You're kidding."

"Does it sound like I'm kidding? I'm serious. If necessary, have a relapse."

"That would be dishonest. I wouldn't dream of tricking Dan like that."

"Of course you wouldn't. Dan knows you would never pull a stunt like that. That's why it would work."

Daniel

Liza sent me a little calendar with a red circle around the date she expects my answer. How insensitive can she get! She knows what I've been going through as father, mother, chief cook and bottle-washer—making the girls' lunches, hiring someone to clean; handling the laundry, the drycleaning, the supermarket; taking Maggie for therapy, the girls for their lessons.

Sonia has surprised me. I thought she of all people would pitch in and help. Instead, she suggests, "Wouldn't Maggie be better off at the Betty Ford Center?"

I'm too tired to discuss it. As a matter of fact, I wish the old bat would retire. I used to make excuses for Sonia—a tough old bird, tactless maybe, but at heart a good woman who treated me like the son she never had.

Forget it. She's a selfish old harridan. She's made Maggie miserable for years. When she asked if she could visit, I said the doctor's order was no excitement.

"How's Liza? When's the wedding, Dan?" Sonia gets right to the point.

Liza seems fine during our brief meetings. We have not discussed personal matters, which explains why she sent me the calendar. She doesn't need to remind me. I know the date. The ultimatum is her idea, not mine.

The fact is, I haven't changed my mind about her or us or the baby. I love her, I want to marry her, but all in good time. I thought I knew her. How can she expect me to leave my family in the lurch? I can't ditch Maggie in her condition. I wouldn't do that to a dog.

I'm doing my best to make Liza understand. You'd think she'd be happy that her future husband has a sense of responsibility. What if *she* gets sick after we're married? Won't she want me to be right there?

Rosalind

Can you beat it? She can't confide in her own mother. What am I, a monster? Did she think I was going to bite off her head and send her out barefoot in a snowstorm?

"Why did I have to get the news from Mark?"

"I was going to tell you, Mother. Honest. I haven't decided what I'm going to do."

"Well, you better get a move-on. Time marches on."

"What would you suggest, an abortion?"

"Are you out of your mind? My own grandchild? I've waited a long time to be a grandmother, thanks to you. I'm talking weddings. I don't want my grandchild to be illegitimate."

"Lighten up, Rosalind. Your favorite movie stars have illegitimate babies. Glenn Close got the Academy Award."

"Sure, and you know what happened to her at the end of the movie, don't you?"

I'm kidding, but she hung up on me, my own daughter.

She made me promise not to interfere, not to call Dan. But I had my fingers crossed. After all, I can't make things worse than they are now.

Liza

It's all getting to be too much. I can't sleep. I can't concentrate. I can't make decisions. Contracts are piling up. There are calls to return. I've run out of juice. All I can think about is Dan, and I hate it. I hate having my life depend on someone else's whim. But it's not a whim. I know it's not a whim. Poor guy, he's caught between the hard place and the hard place. But I mustn't allow myself to feel sorry for him. He's a big boy.

I hate to admit it, but this morning when we were on the phone and he was telling me how much Sandi and Jennifer need him and how Maggie keeps writing him little love-notes thanking him for his kindness, I suddenly got the unpleasant impression that he's loving every minute. He's the hero of this ridiculous soap opera. Torn between two women—the timid little sparrow of a wife who worships and adores him and has devoted her life to the holes in his socks, and the marauding hawk who stole him out of his snug little nest and showed him how to spread his wings and fly high. I'm forgetting Sonia. Three women. And Jennifer and Sandi. Five women. He's the sun-god, and we're the satellites revolving around him, vying for his attention.

He complains, but I can see he's getting off on it; to him it's a thrill a minute. He's king of the mountain, and all our little upturned faces are begging, *Pick me. Pick me.*

I love him. But if necessary, I can live without him. He has exactly three days to make up his mind. I had another letter from the Belgravia lothario. I wonder how he'll react when I say I'm preggers. I've heard that some men groove on screwing pregnant women.

Maggie

Some flowers arrived today from Freddy, with a beautiful get-well card. Inside he wrote, "I know a way to make you feel better but fast. Love, Freddy." I left the card on the dresser so Dan couldn't miss it.

"You seem to have an admirer."

"Just Freddy. He felt sorry for the poor abandoned wife and took me out a few times." (Once, but who's counting?)

"He's had eyes for you for a long time. I could see it the night you had the committee meeting here."

Dan was jealous. How could I make him more jealous?

"Well, as a matter of fact, he made a play for me. He thinks we'd make a terrific couple."

"And how do you feel about that?" My husband was no longer teasing.

"What's sauce for the goose is sauce for the gander. And Freddy's a pretty saucy gander."

Daniel

Jennifer has shown me an article from an old copy of *People* magazine. It's about a twelve-year-old girl described as "the hottest preteen model since Brooke Shields." Richard Avedon photographs her, she's been on the covers of thirteen magazines, and according to her agent, she earns thirty-five hundred dollars a day.

"You see, Daddy? I can do that, too."

She wants to go and see Liza. She reminds me of what Liza said to her that day in the park, that she would arrange some test shots.

"Oh, baby. That was just talk. You're very pretty. It was something to say."

"She meant it. You know she meant it. You've always said I can't take a bad picture. Please, Daddy. Call her."

"I can't do that. Your mother wouldn't like it. You saw how upset she got in the park."

"Please, Daddy. It's my big chance. We don't have to tell her."

"She's not well, you know that. Think how she'll feel if you get together with Liza!"

"What's the difference? She's going to be my stepmother, isn't she?"

Neither of us has noticed the door of Jennifer's room opening. Maggie stands there, swaying and screaming, "Who? Who's going to be your stepmother?"

When I finally calm her down and get her back to bed, Maggie says, "You've got to do something about Jennifer. She's becoming incorrigible. Her marks are way down. She says she hates school and that college is for the birds. She showed me a marijuana cigarette some boy gave her. He's a dealer, she says. He can get heroin and crack. I haven't wanted to tell you. You've got enough problems with me. But it's serious, Dan. She's thirteen going on thirty. Yesterday, she said she could probably make a fortune as a porno star. They like young girls."

There is one thing more she can't hide much longer. Jennifer has run up over five hundred dollars in phone charges, calling those party line numbers.

Maggie doesn't have to tell me. I know. When it comes to divorce, it's the children who suffer the most.

Liza

Today's the day. This is it, kids. Dan is coming for drinks at seven. I can't tell anything from his voice. He sounds tired but good. His voice still sends heat through my body. I know he's been under a lot of strain. In fact, I sent him a carton of stress tablet vitamins—a joke, but serious.

I've hated putting the screws on him like this, but I can't hang around waiting. Like Peggy said that day in Los Angeles, there's always something. After a certain point, no man is worth waiting for. I knew I was taking a risk giving him an ultimatum. It's been an ultimatum for me, too. If I back down now, I'm dead. He'll lose all respect for me. The situation will drag on for years, and in the end, I'll be the one sitting at home the day of his daughter's wedding, or holding his hand at the hospital while Maggie has a menopause baby. Definitely not my scene.

I feel lucky today. Things are really going my way. I can't let this dinky little personal problem affect my business. The accountant met me for breakfast this morning. Liza Central is in deep trouble, he said. We're growing much too fast. It's time to restructure. He wants projections for the next five years and a new business plan. He wants to apply for some major financing. I don't need it now, but I will. He wants the money in place so when I do need it, it'll be there waiting.

A business like mine, or any business for that matter, can't stay in one place. Either it grows or it declines. I can't argue with him. We need more space, more people, more state-of-the-art equipment. My original concept for a small, lean roster was sentimental. Like Marlon Brando said, it was "a one-way ticket to Palookaville."

There's so much to consider. Expansion is not only office space and computer terminals. It's employee benefits, health plans, insurance. He thinks we're spending too much on phone lines and messenger services and has some thoughts about that. A profit-sharing plan might be worth considering, too. It gives key personnel a stake in the business.

That's something Dan and I have discussed. He and Sonia have been through it. They transformed what was once a small carriage-trade travel agency catering to the family of means into a vertical full-service powerhouse. The way Dan explains his approach, he's got one corporate account, where he books all their conferences and high-level travel, which also takes care of summer study programs and teen bus tours for their kids.

I need Dan in every part of my life, a man I can love and whose judgment I value and trust. I can feel it in my bones. He's started the divorce. It's all working out. This morning, I woke up sick to my stomach. I'm not sure if it's nerves or the little stranger. My gynie appointment is next week. I think I'll ask Dan to come with me. After all, he is the father.

Daniel

She took it much better than I expected—no scenes, no name-calling, very matter-of-fact. For a minute, I thought maybe she hadn't understood what I'd said.

"I understand perfectly, Dan. You have not filed for the divorce."

"We've got to talk."

"There's nothing to talk about."

"Please, Liza. Listen to me. I need more time. Maggie's in therapy. It'll take time, but the prognosis is good. She's joined AA, too; not that she's really an alcoholic, but she has an addictive personality and she's taking a positive attitude—dammit, you're not listening!"

She let me have it straight. The state of my wife's health was of minimal interest. She wished Maggie a speedy recovery on principle. She hates to see any other human being suffer. There's too much suffering in the world.

As for us, she had meant what she said. It had been nice knowing me. She thought a clean break was the best. She did not want to see me again or hear from me.

"What about our baby?"

"You mean my baby?"

"Our baby, Liza. I'll—sue you for paternal rights!"

Her look of withering contempt should be patented. I felt about three inches tall.

"And just how do you propose to prove the baby is yours? I'm a liberated woman, you know. I can think of several men who could be the father."

She said her decision was final, and to sum up: She never wanted to see me again; the baby was her business; and if I interfered in any way, she'd get a cease-and-desist court order against me.

"Goodbye and good luck, Dan. I'm sorry it didn't work out. Better luck next time."

I can't believe I'll never see her again. Never hold her in my arms. Maggie is very understanding. She didn't ask me where I was going. When I got back, she didn't ask me where I'd been. I think she had some inkling. She looked relieved when I returned.

I can't talk about it for the moment. Tomorrow, I'll check out of the hotel. My things are still there. I haven't been there since Maggie's breakdown. In a few days I'll feel better. I've got to get a grip on myself. If I tell Maggie now, I'm afraid I'll burst into tears.

Maggie

Jennifer thinks I should get a perm. She wants to go with me to Bloomingdale's to pick out a nice wardrobe. She's all excited about my new job. A friend of Dan's has a friend who sent me along to another friend who got me a job on the new fashion magazine, *Clothes Horse.* I caution Jennifer that I'm not the editor—only a glorified office girl is what they said. But Jennifer is firmly convinced I will get them to use her as a model.

"We'll show that Liza, won't we, Mom?"

We've already shown her. We're lucky to be a family again. "We don't have to get even with anyone, dear. Liza fell in love with Daddy. How could she help herself? He's the smartest, handsomest, bestest man in the entire world."

He's past the worst of it, I think. Helen says no matter what, *never* say anything derogatory about Liza. He can if he wants to. You can't. You must never put him in the position of defending her.

"Forget the past, Maggie. Don't dwell on what he did or said. Don't throw it in his face. It might make you feel good to see him sweat. It's not worth it. Forgive him so he can forgive himself."

I've just completed my three-day seminar in self-esteem. I'm out of Valium, but the pharmacist knows me and refilled the prescription. I thought I would clean out the safe-deposit box, but when I saw how much cash I've stashed away and the pictures of Liza, I decided to leave them where they are. Dan would appreciate my position. One of his all-time favorites is Louis Armstrong: *One never know, do one?*

Liza

I'm up to my ears in work. My mother showed up at the office with two jars of rhubarb and strawberries and a package of plastic cups.

"I'm not staying. I just thought—"

I'd never seen her like this. I followed her to the ladies' room. "Rosalind—"

"Don't call me Rosalind. I'm your mother. I just want you to know you can count on me no matter what." She pats my stomach, hugs me and nearly cracks a rib, and makes a run for it before I can hug her back.

I had dinner with Mark last night. I never thought we could be friends, but that seems to be what's happening—another example of how strange life can be. We've agreed to a truce about the past, no more recriminations. We're becoming confidantes, something both of us need in our lives. I can talk to him about business and his eyes don't glaze over. He's interested in details. He knows about money. He's made some tax-structuring suggestions that will save me a bundle.

With our past finally behind us, he feels comfortable discussing his personal life and asking my advice. Listening to him is an education in cross-purposes. I was married to the man, yet it's astounding to see how naive he is about women. His latest, for instance, the shrink. He was deeply impressed by her instant analysis of him. He was utterly enthralled. This woman could have sold him the Brooklyn Bridge. It bothered me that she might have told him to jump off it, and he might have done it as an act of personal courage.

As it turns out, I needn't have worried. Last night he told me they'd split. "I should have seen it coming. She said she wanted a ski house. I'm a pleasant fellow. I said it sounded like a good idea. She said her birthday was coming up, and it would be nice if I bought one for her as a gift. Not as a loan, mind you, no hint of paying me back or of joint ownership. We're talking major moola here. She was so sure of herself, she suggested flying to Switzerland this weekend."

"Is that what you call a snow job?"

"Oh, Liza. What would I do if I didn't have you to tell my troubles to?"

"And vice versa, Mark."

I extended the pinkie finger of my right hand to him. He hooked his matching finger into mine. We shook three times, a ritual holdover from a city playground childhood—"Friends for life."

I'm feeling a lot better about things. My gynie appointment is this afternoon. A few minutes ago, Mark phoned to thank me for last night and to ask if I wanted him to accompany me to the doctor's.

"I'm fine, Mark, really. I'd rather go alone."

That's when he offered to marry me. "I've been up all night thinking about it. We've been through the wars, Liza. We could both do a lot worse. We'd be giving the baby a name."

He was being sweet and caring, but he still doesn't understand. If I have the baby, it will be my baby, and it will have my name.

Daniel

I can't stop thinking about the baby. I don't care what she says, it's my baby, too. I'm entitled to know what's happening.

Myrna says she's at the doctor's.

"The gynecologist? Is she okay?"

"She was when she left here ten minutes ago."

She's in the waiting room when I arrive.

"What are you doing here?" she demands.

The other women look up from their magazines expectantly—no pun intended. We're a domestic quarrel about to explode.

"I'm expecting a baby." Good comeback, if I say so myself.

"If you don't get out of here this minute, I'll have you thrown out." But her sense of humor gets the better of her. "The nurse is bigger than you are. She'll break you in half."

Said nurse appears on cue. The doctor is ready. I make it clear that I will be waiting until she comes out.

The waiting room is stuffy, the Mantovani music smooth. I must have fallen asleep, because the next thing I know Liza streaks past me through the door and into the street. She has crossed Park Avenue against the lights and is halfway to Madison when I catch up with her.

"Liza! What happened?"

"I'm not pregnant!"

"Please, Liza—tell me—"

"I got my period right there. Like turning a faucet. All over his nice examining table. Okay? Is that what you wanted to know? You can go home now. Leave me alone."

"Are you okay?"

"No, Dan. I am not okay. Are you?"

Maggie

Dan didn't show up for dinner and didn't call. My heart was in my mouth. *Please, not again!* He strolled in near midnight. Without a word, he got undressed as if I weren't there.

"Dan—"

He emptied his pockets and folded his trousers neatly over the back of the chair.

"Dan—where were you? We were so worried. You might have had the decency to call."

He removed his watch and began to examine it as if it were a strange object he'd never seen before. Using both hands, he pulled the stretch band as far as it would go and let it snap back. As an afterthought, he stretched the band again until it broke.

"Dan! For God's sake—"

"Please don't shout, Maggie. I can hear you."

"Then why don't you answer me when I speak to you?

Where were you tonight? With her? With Liza! That's where you were, screwing that—"

"Don't say it, Maggie. Don't say another word."

He sat down beside me on the bed and took my hand.

"I'm telling you for the last time. I will never see Liza again."

He gathers me into his arms.

"Don't worry. We're going to be fine."

Liza

It wasn't my imagination. I had all the symptoms—the skipped period, the bloat, the tender breasts. The morning nausea. The doctor says I may have spontaneously miscarried or may never have been pregnant at all.

"I wasn't making it up."

It was a common occurrence, he assured me, among career women especially. The stress of travel, jogging, diet, all the emotional problems of the workplace often affect the menstrual cycle. He didn't think there was any other problem. My last pap smear had been negative. The flow appeared normal. My belly was distended but would go away. He wanted me back for a checkup in ten days, just to be sure.

There's nothing wrong with me. Not now. I'm free as the birds in the trees and flying just as high. In a way, I'm glad Dan was at the doctor's office. It saved me from having to decide whether to tell him or not. I mustn't be too hard on him. A man's got to do what a man's got to do. Just as long as he doesn't do it to me.

On balance, I'm more sad than sorry—the old might-havebeens. I wanted that baby. More to the point, I want *a* baby. My sex drive has come back with a vengeance. I'm Randy Mandy, so hot I could hump doorknobs. I want *sex.* With Mark. With the Belgravia lothario. With that cute cop on the corner. I don't *care!* I'll take any one of them. *All* of them!

Women are basically more erotic than men and much more complex in sexual response. Thinking back to good old Mark, I remember what happened when I first heard rumors that he was having real breakfasts with an actual Tiffany. I thought the best defense was a good offense and took the sex-kitten route—garter belt, net stockings, no-crotch panties, baby oil, incense, the whole enchilada.

The man went nuts. He reacted like a battery-operated sex doll, ricocheting off the walls like a demented pinball. I remember feeling strangely disassociated, like I had stumbled into somebody else's movie; and I felt a little maternal, too, like I was providing a special treat for my oafish baby boy.

As for Dan, he's too recent to forget. I manage not to think about him at all. Funnily enough, the ones I do think about are Jennifer and Sandi. Jennifer—that pouting, angry little face, so fierce, so hungry for love and life. I wish I could have helped her to do some modeling, not as a career but for the fun of it and to make a few dollars for college or travel. That little Sandi I could easily scoop up and take home. That day when we took them to the Hard Rock, we were walking along Fifty-seventh Street when Sandi reached for my hand and called me "Mommy." She realized in a flash that I wasn't Maggie, but she hung onto my hand anyway.

What I want is a daughter of my own, someone to nurture and educate and teach about taupe eye shadow and the pleasures of museums. Being honest with myself, I won't be too particular who the father is, so long as he's nice and healthy and generous of spirit.

The Belgravia lothario may be just the ticket. He arrives next week. He'll be on my turf. It will be interesting to see how he plays in my backyard.

Tonight, I'm home and grateful to be alone. I find it therapeutic to straighten my drawers: panty hose are sorted by colors and condition—I keep separate the ones with runs to wear under slacks. Scarves go by size and fabric. Gloves. I don't know how I've accumulated so many pairs of gloves. They reproduce themselves in the darkness of night, except for one genetic fault—they're all left-hands and only good for clutching along with your program at a concert.

My technique is to dump the entire contents of the glove drawer on the bed. Something glistens—Dan's zircon "engagement" ring, which I thought I had lost accidentally on purpose. He's a gentleman, is Dan. He didn't ask for it back. The bedroom window beckons. I toss it as high and as far as I can. The zircon glints like a falling star. It wasn't worth much, just six months of my life.

It's dinner time. I know I should be eating something high in vitamins and minerals and low in saturated fats. For once in my life, I'm not hungry. No secret cravings for greaseburgers and cottage fries, heavy on the ketchup. Tonight I shall be like an Eskimo, my body fueling itself on its own fat. The idea appeals to me, and I am wondering if I can lose enough fat overnight to get into a size eight, when the phone rings.

"Hi."

"Hi, Mark."

"You okay?"

"Uh-huh. You?"

"I've got something to tell you."

"Don't tell me. You bought her the ski house!"

"Liza! Come on—"

"I'm sorry. What?"

"I found the Ferlinghetti!"

"You skunk. You had it all along."

"No—I swear—it was stuck inside that giant book of film classics. I must have put it there when I looked something up. Believe me, I didn't steal it."

"I believe you."

"You're sure?"

"In fact, you can keep it. It's okay. Really."

"No. It's yours. I insist on returning it. What are you doing about dinner?"

"Nothing."

"Want to come out?"

"I'm tired. I'm in for the night."

"Want me to bring something over?"

"I'm not hungry."

"You've got to eat."

"You sound like my mother."

"I'm better than that. I'm your friend. How about I pick up some pasta salad and a nice cold bottle of wine?"

"I look awful, Mark. My hair's a mess. I'm wearing my ratty old terrycloth robe."

"You mean *my* ratty old terrycloth robe, remember?"

"I remember." The truth? I had forgotten. I have a closet full of robes, but this is my favorite. And it *had* belonged to Mark.

"Come on now, Liza. Concentrate. What do you want to eat?"

"Surprise me."

I'm beginning to feel better. I tie back my hair in a silk

paisley scarf and apply a few deft touches of no-makeup makeup to enhance my wan but wonderful languor. *Courage, Camille.* Armand Duval is about to arrive with a basket of *marrons glaces.* I hate *marrons glaces.* They're like soap erasers covered with glue. I hope Mark brings something better than that. I am feeling much better by the time he arrives with the battered Ferlinghetti and a familiar shopping bag from Zabar's.

"Guess what I got you?"

"Oh, Mark—you remembered!"

It's nostalgia time at the old corral. I settle into the sofa with my legs tucked under and the terrycloth wrapped around, munching the cheese Danish and sipping the hot chocolate while Mark reads aloud from the Ferlinghetti.

> I am waiting
> for a rebirth of wonder

I feel content with Mark being here. Yet I know I would feel just as content if he were not. I think of all that has happened and all that may lie ahead, and I wonder if I am at a crossroads or have simply hit a few bumps on a long, straight road, or whether what goes around really does come around.

As Mark continues to read, I feel a wild and sudden surge of gratitude for the triumphs of work and the raptures of love, while all the time mindful of time running out and my gnawing impatience as I, too, wait for a rebirth of wonder.